Orphea Proud

ALSO BY SHARON DENNIS WYETH

The World of Daughter McGuire

A Piece of Heaven

Something Beautiful

Always My Dad

Once on This River

SHARON DENNIS WYETH

Orphea Proud

DELACORTE PRESS

Published by
Delacorte Press
an imprint of
Random House Children's Books
a division of Random House, Inc.
New York

Visit us on the Web! www.randomhouse.com/teens
Educators and librarians, for a variety of teaching tools, visit us at
www.randomhouse.com/teachers

Library of Congress Cataloging-in-Publication Data
Wyeth, Sharon Dennis.
Orphea Proud / Sharon Dennis Wyeth.
p. cm.
Summary: While reciting her poetry at a club in Queens, New York,
seventeen-year-old Orphea recounts her childhood in Pennsylvania, leaving
after her parents and the girl she loves die, and learning about her family and
herself while living with her great-aunts on a Virginia mountaintop.
ISBN 0-385-32497-9 (trade) — ISBN 0-385-90175-5 (GLB)
[1. Family life—Fiction. 2. Poetry—Fiction. 3. Lesbians—Fiction.
4. Artists—Fiction. 5. Entertainers—Fiction. 6. Racially mixed people—
Fiction. 7. Queens (New York, N.Y.)—Fiction.] I. Title.
PZ7.W9746Or 2004
[Fic]—dc22
2003022727

The text of this book is set in 12.25-point Apollo MT.

Book design by Angela Carlino

Printed in the United States of America

November 2004

10 9 8 7 6 5 4 3 2 1

BVG

For Georgia

Acknowledgments

Sincere thanks to my editor, Michelle Poploff, for her keen insight and extraordinary patience. I also appreciate assistant editor Joe Cooper's input. The optimism and friendship of my agent, Robin Rue, were of inestimable value as always. There are others who lent me support during this project, either through reading various versions of the manuscript or through discussion of its themes: Harriet Weitzner, psychologist Thelma Markowitz, Mimi Leahey, Eiko Otake, Bonnie Reed, Amber Reed, Dr. M. Jerry Weiss, Nancy Plain, Dr. Diane Klein, and P-Flag of North Jersey. My husband, Sims, is the steady flame in my life. My daughter, Georgia, continues to inspire me.

Orphea Proud

"It's your movie."

That's what Lissa would say.

Meaning, it's my life and I should be the one to control it.

But what if on a perfect snow day, you just don't think about what will happen when you make love with your best friend while your asshole brother is downstairs in the kitchen with a glass to the ceiling, listening for every whisper, every squeak in the bed? There's no control then—because love isn't about control.

Love is the one place where we have to lose it.

Hot ice
Taboo to the touch
A fire in the cold
That was us

Showtime

"**Don't** look back."

That's what they told me.

So I won't turn around, even though I'm itching to. I want to see what that skinny little pale dude up on the ladder is painting behind my back. But I can't, because I have to look at you. You're the audience, after all. And I'm the performer. Raynor Grimes, the guy up on the ladder, well, he's part of the performance, too, but he doesn't talk, he paints, which means he keeps his eyes on his gargantuan canvas, while I keep my eyes on you. Without you none of us would be here, not me or Ray or Mr. Icarus Digits, the owner of this

3

club, or Marilyn Chin, your waitress this evening who plays the electric bass and whose eyes look like they're bleeding on account of her burgundy mascara.

Welcome to our show!—which we've kind of nicknamed *Not a Rodeo,* for reasons I'll tell you later.

I'm Orphea Proud.

For those of you who've never been here, welcome to Club Nirvana!—a former meat warehouse. Some people say it stinks here. Once upon a time slabs of beef did hang from the ceiling. During the day, the place *is* dank, a nondescript square carved out of shitty concrete with the faint smell of pig's entrails. But at night, the space transforms. When I step inside this club before the show, the walls hug me. The people here are my little family. I bump my butt up onto the stage and Icky Digits waves at me from the light booth. If it weren't for Icky, I'd be sitting in a diner staring at an egg yolk, thinking it's a sunflower. When I get here in the evening, I see Raynor Grimes, too. Ray always arrives before I do, even though we live together. He scurries on over to mix his paints in private. Sometimes if I sneak in early, I spy. This evening I spotted a thin layer of ethereal blue. And I thought, oh yeah what a backdrop! Maybe tonight Ray's painting will be all *me*—study of a big-booty poet against a pale blue sky.

I said that the people at Club Nirvana are like my family. In fact Raynor and I are blood related. Something I didn't know when I first met him on top of a mountain down in Virginia. You're wondering how a vanilla boy with straw-colored hair could be kin to a coffee girl like me? Sure you are. Not only that, he's so skinny, his shoulder blades stick through his shirt like angel's wings—whereas I have meat on my bones. Never know who might be in your family, ain't it the truth?

Who else can I tell you about? Your waitress and my good friend Marilyn Chin! Besides playing bass and having a thing for burgundy mascara, Marilyn reads tea leaves. After the show, she'll read yours if you ask her. I warn you, though, her readings can be puzzling. When Ray and I first came to Queens, New York, to do our show and stay with her and Icky, Marilyn read mine.

"You are in grave danger of being devoured."

"Devoured by what?"

"Words. They will eat you like maggots."

"So, is there any way I can avoid this horrendous fate?"

"Sure," Marilyn said. "Make a raft of them."

Hmm, a raft of words. . . . Maybe you can figure that one out.

Next up—Mr. Icarus Digits! He wasn't always a club owner. He used to cook short-order in a diner in the town in Pennsylvania where I grew up. The diner had an open-mike night on Fridays. I started going when I was twelve and never missed a Friday after that. Being able to hear poets and musicians was like opening the iron bars of my prison. I was living with my brother, Rupert, and his wife in a house where I found it hard to breathe. But on Friday nights at the diner, I could throw open the doors inside myself and let poetry and music whistle through me while I felt all kinds of stuff; delicious stuff and scary stuff and parts of myself that I had not yet come to love. Another reason I was drawn to the diner was that I was already into writing poetry myself. But when I first went to the open-mike night, I just listened. One day, Icky Digits spotted me from behind the counter where he was cooking and encouraged me to get up and perform. My friend Lissa was there to encourage me, too, or I should say she nagged me. My first performance at the mike was the beginning of something taking shape inside me; a sense that I'd be a poet for the rest of my life and maybe even a performer. Icky Digits was right there with me, helping to make it possible, just like he's made it possible for me and Ray to put on our show at Club Nirvana these past few weeks. Want to hear something awesome about Icky Digits? He has no fingerprints. He won't tell me why. Maybe he tossed too much hot stuff at the grill or got too close to some lights. He's obsessed with theatrical lighting—he won't mind me saying that. He likes me bathed in pink. But sometimes he'll switch to red or blue. So expect me to keep changing colors. And look out—he's been known to throw a spotlight on the audience. Icky has one other interest, t'ai chi, which he practices every morning, advancing like a slow wind through the loft. Ray and I just ignore him and go on eating our cereal. Marilyn usually misses out on Icky's t'ai chi routine, because she takes such a long time in the bathroom.

So, that's the gang at Club Nirvana. Did I leave anyone out?

Yeah . . . You.

You're a very sexy audience. I love the way you laugh. I bet you can dance on the ceiling and eat pretzels off the floor with one hand tied behind you. Admit it—you're an adrenaline junkie, undulating hysteria about to explode, waiting to be discovered. You're not cynical, are you? Please tell me you're not. But if you are, I guess it's okay. I've had my moments, too. But it's hard to be cynical when you're telling a love story. And that's what I'm about to do.

Words rule, baby
Don't let no one tell you otherwise
Lest it be a skinny painter
You don't buy that tale about a tree
How it sprung through the cracks from a seed?
If you do, you're a fool
'Cause the word came first, then that thing with bark
    and leaves
A cow was C-O-W 'fore it could say Moo
And L-O-V-E? A luscious kiss upon earth's tongue,
    waiting for the
Moment to lick and say out loud what we feel in our
    hearts
The heat of mama's hand upon your brow
The firm grip of a friend when you are falling
The javelin energy of lust let loose to make or break you
But first and last, it was all a word

MOM

Okay, you guys—

In the beginning, there was MOM.

Are you with me?

Mom's name was Nadine.

Nadine reached out for every snotty-nosed, scab-kneed part of me. I had a permanent home on her lap. For hours I would lay my cheek in the curve of her shoulder, sniffing at her neck. Her hair was a crown of a thousand black braids to wind my fingers through. She wore an orange silk skirt permanently stained with the chocolate signature of my kiss. Once when I was three, I hugged her around the legs and pressed my mouth to her knee after eating an ice cream cone and Nadine refused to send the skirt to the dry cleaners, so that the imprint of my kiss would always be there.

My mom had a voice as soft as fleece that made you feel warm all over when she spoke to you. But after dinner in the evening when my father and his shadow, my half-grown brother Rupert, would go out on business to the church, my mom would sing along with the radio. She liked the "classics." I can hear her singing "Natural Woman" with Aretha, her voice soaring high and steely above the sound of running water at the sink and the clanking pots and pans.

Nadine was a natural singer, but she'd always dreamed of voice lessons. When the choir director at Daddy's church found out, he and Nadine got into cahoots. She sneaked off to his house on Saturday afternoons on her way from the grocery store, carrying me with her. The choir director had a funny little goatee sprouting out of the middle of his chin. His name was John. I remember how he would take his place on a shiny black bench while Nadine stood facing him, her body leaning into the side of the open grand piano, bags of groceries at her feet. Sheltering me in the crook of her arm, she propped me up next to her so that my behind rested on a precipice above the strings of the instrument. Beneath the shadow of the piano's lid, John's tawny fingers skittered up and down the keyboard, as he led Nadine through her scales. The sound vibrated up my spine. And when my mother hugged me close, and I laid my hand on her throat, I felt the rush of a magic river. Since my ear was next to her chest, I could also hear her heartbeat and the sharp intake of her breathing. After the warm-up exercises, she would sing another kind of classic, a famous aria from the opera *Carmen*.

"*L'amour, l'amour . . .*" Of course, I didn't know what she was singing about at the time, but there was aching in her voice.

If Daddy had known about those lessons, he would have been mad. My father ruled with an iron hand. I was forced to sit for hours at the table in front of a bowl of peas, even after the sight of them made me throw up. So, if you ask me to dinner, don't serve peas. Once when my big brother Rupert was late for his nine o'clock curfew in high school, Daddy switched him with his belt. Though Rupert didn't cry, I was terrified. So when Daddy walked in unexpectedly one day, while Nadine was singing "Natural Woman" along to the radio, and snatched the plug out of the wall and threw the radio into the sink, I hid under the table. But Nadine was so brave. She picked the radio up out of the sink and dried it off without batting an eyelash. Then she actually laughed.

"Are you trying to get through to me, Apollo?"

Daddy still looked angry. Nadine threw her arms around his waist. She gave him a big fat kiss. "You're such a mean ol' man. Don't know why I married you."

"Because I'm the biggest, baddest preacher in these parts." He didn't look angry anymore. Guess that fat kiss did it. He tugged Nadine's hair. "But how's it look having the preacher's wife be so reckless?"

"You ain't seen reckless," Nadine teased. "I'm only singing to the radio, enjoying myself. And look how you scared little Orphea."

Nadine smiled in my direction, but Daddy kept his eyes fixed on her face. "Save that pretty voice for Sunday," he warned. "Next thing I know, you'll be sneaking off to a dance club."

Nadine shook her hips. "Would that be such a crime?" My mom had attitude. As far as I know, she didn't sneak off to a club. But every Saturday we did sneak off to John's for her voice lesson. One of Daddy's rules was that she couldn't wear lipstick, but Nadine wore it then. Lipstick the color of candy apples—I've scoured drugstores for the shade. She also wore black kohl on the bottom lids of her eyes. She'd smile at me in the mirror when she was made up. Then off we'd go to the store to throw the groceries into the cart, then hop back into the car and race over to John's to sing the role of Carmen—with no one in the audience but the piano player and the child in the crook of her arm.

When Nadine sang Carmen, her face lit up so. If Daddy could have seen her, there's no way he could have stayed mad. But he never did catch her singing at John's. He died before he had the chance. One Sunday he fell out of his pulpit and that was the end of him.

"Heart attack." I heard Rupert say it. He was talking to someone on the phone. Our father had a heart attack. Rupert was already in college. He helped

Nadine make the telephone calls. Nadine wasn't his mother. She was only mine. But Daddy belonged to us both. But now he had a heart attack. I was only seven. I didn't know what it meant. My memory of the funeral was sitting next to Nadine at church in an ocean of people. My stomach was queasy, I remember. I asked where Daddy was, a few weeks after he'd gone. The thought of him disappearing was impossible. He was too tall.

"Where did Daddy go?"

"Heaven," Nadine whispered.

"Where's that?"

"In the air."

That sounded right to me. "In the air" was where Daddy had always seemed to be, at least on Sundays, towering above from the pulpit. It was my favorite view of him, because on Sundays when he preached I saw him from the front. At home during the week, I mainly saw only the back of him. His straight back as he walked out the front door of our house on Sherman Court, a very nice house purchased for him with the help of the congregation but which Nadine got to keep. Our house—with a porch and an old-fashioned parlor in place of a living room and lots of bedrooms on the second floor. He and Rupert were always leaving for someplace important, not always the church, sometimes the car wash. But on Sundays when he preached, I saw Daddy's face, its thick gray eyebrows and burning eyes. I saw his long arms waving while his voice boomed down, warning the people to be good or else be sorry. And then one day he went to Heaven, to be permanently in the air.

At the end of that year Rupert graduated. Nadine and I went to see him wearing his cap and gown. He had a girlfriend named Ruby hanging on his arm. She was wearing a blue dress with white flowers. When she said hello, instead of looking at us, she looked at her pale yellow shoes.

Rupert got in Nadine's face right away. "Why are you here?"

"The school mailed an announcement."

"That would have been meant for my father."

She smiled. "We're your family, too. You graduated with honors. We're proud of you."

"You ain't my family," he snapped. "But since you're here, you might as well sit down. You'll have to hold *her* on your lap, though. The other seat is for Ruby."

On the ride home from Rupert's school, Nadine got a headache that nothing would help. She woke up with it for months after. As far as I know she never went to a doctor, even though it meant she had to stop reading to me at night. She said the words seemed double. So I read instead, choosing the book she liked best, an easy-to-read one about a duck named Ping. She smiled while I read. She smiled a lot. Her very last smile that I remember was the following spring, on a day when we went to a fair. She let me go up on the Ferris wheel all by myself. She was afraid it would make her dizzy. So I got on alone. I felt as if I were flying. I also felt very grown-up. We'd lied to the Ferris

14

wheel guy and said I was ten; I was tall for my age. But when I reached the tippy-top, I felt eight years old and real short. I began to panic. I looked down at the crowd. I saw Mom immediately. Her eyes were on me and she was smiling. Right away I felt calm. Soon after the fair, Nadine went to the hospital. After that she went into the ground. . . .

■ ■ ■

As they lowered my mother's coffin into the pit, I tried to break away. We were far from home. I saw a mountain. We had buried Daddy behind his church. But Nadine wanted to be buried with her people.

Rupert grabbed my wrist. "Be still."

They eased the coffin lower. The earth was swallowing her.

I whimpered.

"Hush," said Ruby.

Rupert tightened his grip. I bit him. He yelped and I jerked free. In one giant twirl, I was riding the coffin, my arms stretched across the top, my face impaled on the roses.

"Mom!"

A gasp went through the crowd. They probably thought that I was trying to kill myself. But I was only trying to rescue Nadine. I would brush the flowers and dirt off of the coffin and open it. Nadine would be there, wearing candy-apple-red lipstick and black kohl on the bottom lid of her eyes.

"Fooled you! I'm not dead! Orphea guessed I was alive. Orphea is sharp as a tack!"

Then she'd hug me. That's all I was after. For one last hug, I threw myself into the pit. But before I could open the coffin, someone picked me up.

■　■　■

I was eight years old when that happened. Rupert was twenty-two. He and Ruby got married and became my guardians. Ruby moved in with us and she and Rupert took over Nadine and Daddy's bedroom. Ruby stayed home to take care of me. Rupert told me that Ruby's presence in the house was a great luxury that I should be thankful for. Not too many kids lose their mothers and get them replaced so quickly. Rupert said Ruby had given things up; the deal had been that she could keep going to college when they got married. Because of me, she went to college at night. In the evenings when she left, she tried giving me hugs. But I didn't like Ruby's neck. Ruby's neck smelled like talcum. Nadine's neck smelled like herself.

That was also the year I stopped seeing in color.

■ ■ ■

To say is
To fall upon the knife
To bleed
Fresh tears
To feed the flowers

■ ■ ■

LISSA

So that's where I was at when I met Lissa. When my parents died, a gray fog hijacked my mind, leaving me to look out at the world through an unwashed window. Then Lissa came along. I was ten and so was she.

The first time I saw her, she was flying a kite. Ruby had sent me to the park. The wind was fierce that day, biting. I stuffed my hands through the holes in my pockets, trying to warm them on my thighs. My lips were chapped.

Lissa had long, thick hair; it, like the kite, was being tossed in every direction. She held on to the ball of string. The kite was so high in the sky; a shadow diving through the clouds like a lost bird. I thought for sure that the wind would tear it, or that the string would break. But Lissa wrestled it toward home, bracing her back against a tree as tall as a castle, fighting to recapture the taut string, winding until her hands burned, until the kite collapsed into the tree's branches.

My heart sank. I could see now that the kite was a fish, lost forever, skewered on a bough. But then she began to climb the tree, which was probably fifty feet high, and she got to the spot where the kite was and brought it back down. By then I was standing beneath the tree myself. Her cheeks were tearstained and her nose was running. It was so windy, but I'd forgotten the cold. She held out the kite for me to see and smiled. One of her bottom teeth was missing. I smiled back. Then she reached into her pocket and took out a tissue and tore it and gave me half.

"You climbed really high," I said, wiping my nose.

"I had to get my kite."

"Weren't you afraid to fall?"

"No."

We stared at each other. I could see myself reflected in her eyes.

"What's your name?" I shuffled my feet.

"Lissa, silly."

"Mine's Orphea."

"I know."

"You do?"

"You're on my bus."

"I am?"

"I sit in back."

"I didn't see you."

"That's 'cause you sit in front."

I tried hard to remember. How could the girl who climbed trees so high be on my bus? I stared at her beautiful hair and my memory jogged. The shiny hair bobbing, the last one off, something in her hand . . . "Do you have a stuffed mole with sunglasses? You take to school?"

"And you have a stuffed dolphin."

"Yes!"

"Told you you're on my bus."

She smiled her crooked smile again. She talked with a really cool lisp. She stuck my hand into one of her pockets. We walked across the park.

"Orphea is an unusual name."

She used a big word. She was smart.

"Where did it come from?"

"My mom named me after a guy named Orpheus. He was a singer a long, long time ago."

"In-ter-resting. Do you like to sing?"

"I sing like a frog."

She giggled.

"My mom liked to sing," I added, "but not anymore."

"How come?"

"She died."

"So that's why you're sad?"

"I'm not sad."

"You're not?"

"I was. But not anymore."

And with that, my world brightened. She wore a red coat that day. The torn kite in her hand was turquoise.

She wrinkled her nose. "Do you like dolls?"

"No, I hate them."

The next day on the bus, I saw her. She had traded up to the middle. By the end of the week, I had traded back and we were sitting side by side.

From then on, Lissa and I were hooked at the pinky. We shared peanut butter and jelly in the lunchroom and parkas on the playground. We did a science project together—a rock collection that we put together at her house. Her parents were white, but race didn't seem to come into it. As a matter of fact, Lissa's father, Mr. Evans, had fixed Daddy's car. Daddy had taken it to Mr. Evans's garage. So our two families kind of knew each other. Guess that's why Ruby and Rupert let me stay over for supper at Lissa's house sometimes. When Mrs. Evans cooked, Lissa and I helped by buttering bread or setting the table or putting the water on to boil potatoes. I helped Lissa surprise her family once by making a cake all by ourselves. By mistake we left out sugar and sweetened it with salt.

Lissa and I listened to the same music, rap and a string of folk singers—she taught me to dance every morning to wake myself up. Not that we did too much sleeping on our sleepovers. We talked until we passed out, sprawled across the same bed with all our clothes on. Who had time to spread out a sleeping bag or change to pajamas, when there were secrets to share? She was the one I called when I got my first period. The one I told how much I missed Nadine. She was my best friend in the world. She wrapped my soul in golden ribbons.

Then came the year we were sixteen.

■ ■ ■

It was a perfect snow day. White light fell across my bed, forcing the colors in the quilt to pop like a field of sunflowers. My cheek was still warm from the pillow. Our toes were touching. Our knees rose separately beneath the covers to make four separate mountains. When we were younger, we'd stretch our legs up, too, and make a teepee. I could hear her breathing. On other snow days, we'd pulled on snow pants to get ready for sledding. We'd read ourselves into exhaustion and make ourselves sick with hot chocolate and marshmallows. We'd pummel each other with snowballs and shovel the neighbors' walks for a quarter.

Now, at sixteen, we stayed in bed . . . touching. I reached over her chest and turned up the radio. She grabbed my hand. I stroked her hair. She held me oh so tightly. We gazed into each other's laughing eyes. We kissed and kissed again. From my head to my toes, I was melting. The night we'd spent had been so surprising, for us both . . . and yet so natural. We had covered every inch of ground together, why not this? My mind began to spin and when I closed my eyes, I could still see the hanging on my wall from Kenya that had once been Nadine's. Blood red woven cloth, shot with gold, it stared down as our only witness, along with the white light flooding the window. . . .

Rupert knocked. I didn't hear him. Without waiting, he opened the door to my room. I looked up. He stood there, frozen, staring. For an instant we were frozen, too, our arms and legs entangled, in the sheets and quilt, entangled with each other.

Then he lurched across the room and grabbed me by the hair. Lissa crawled over one of my legs, taking the quilt with her, slipping onto the floor with a barely audible scream. Out of the corner of my eye, I caught a glimpse of her, as I went flying. Rupert had found the strength in his scrawny body to pick me up, to yank me up out of the bed. Before throwing me across the room, he shook me. Even though I'm as tall as he is and I'm sure that I'm stronger, because he's all flab and no muscles, his hatred of me in that moment gave him the strength. And I was too stunned to summon my own forces. Just like the time at Nadine's funeral, when I'd tried to rescue her from death and someone had picked me up off the coffin and I'd gone limp. It happened again and I couldn't help Lissa, as she struggled toward the door, grabbing her jeans and jacket and knapsack. I couldn't help her, because now Rupert was slamming me up against the wall, butting my head against Nadine's hanging from Kenya. I was crying and could hardly breathe, and the sun that had been so warm and delicious was a floodlight in my eyes and my brother's face looked horrific, like a monster's. Then I heard a real scream and I yanked my head toward the door and Rupert kneed me in the stomach and it wasn't Lissa standing there. Lissa was gone. It was Ruby, holding her arms out, telling her husband to stop.

"Don't," she cried. "Rupert, you'll kill her!"

Everything got quiet and he dropped me.

"You're going to Hell for this," he growled.

If that could have been the end of it, I would have taken two more beatings. I would have offered up an arm or a leg, if only that could have been it. Just Rupert catching us and beating me up and Lissa going home to her parents.

I heard a car revving up outside. I hurried to the window. Lissa was in her van. She was having trouble getting out of the parking space, because of the snow. The tires were spinning and exhaust was filling the air. I opened my window and tried to signal her. At that moment, Rupert came outside.

He went around to the driver's side. Lissa rolled down her window.

He was saying something to her. She listened for only a moment, then peeled off, skidding at last out of the parking spot. Why had Rupert gone after her? What had he said? Hadn't he humiliated us enough?

As if he could read my thoughts, my brother stared up at me with a look that, even from down on the street, told me that as far as he was concerned I was an insect. I had been squashed, I was bleeding and tasting my own blood; my arm was shooting with pain. I found it hard to walk, but when I heard his footsteps on the stairs again, I ran.

I ran across the room and slammed the door, and then I pushed the bed over, and then the dresser and all the other furniture. I barricaded myself in. But I needn't have bothered, because neither Rupert nor Ruby came back. I leaned on the dresser, waiting, straining to hear what was going on, staring at a face in the mirror that belonged to somebody else it was so banged up and so scared.

That morning was the last time I saw her.

Is there a mask in Raynor's sky?
A pulled-down mouth with frightened eyes?
Or has he stabbed the veil of blue with a sharp white
spire?
A black blotch shows the preacher's falling back
A child's cheek appears tattooed with roses
Or is the canvas cut by streaks of red and gold refracted
quilt?
Is there a stain upon the pillow?
Is there a shirt in tatters?
My love's imagined face or as she ran a snake upon her
ankle
There is a chance that Ray has washed it all away
Covering the dream of blue with the dream of gray

GREEN

For my twelfth birthday, Lissa gave me a watercolor. The painting of a leaf, translucent with delicacy, its every vein defined, sharp yet tender at the same time. I hung it on the wall in my room next to the window, so that the light could hit it. When Lissa saw what I had done, she was embarrassed.

"Why are you making such a big deal?"

"I like it."

"It's not a real painting, Orphea."

"What's a real painting?"

"Something by Picasso. If he had painted that leaf, it would be fractured and crooked. If you had gone with my mom and me to the museum in Philadelphia, you'd know what I mean."

"But fractured and crooked sounds ugly."

"Not ugly, cool. You have a Picasso face."

"Gee, thanks."

"Your face is crooked. That's what makes you so beautiful."

"You need new contacts, or else go back to wearing glasses."

"Orphea, you know that you're pretty."

"Shut up."

"You are." She wrapped her pinky around mine and a little shock went through me.

"Your leaf is pretty, too," I said. "Better than anything I could see in a museum."

I was telling the truth. There was something about that leaf. A personal quality, not only because it was for me. That watercolor was something only she could have done. It had her brand on it—know what I mean?

Around that time, Lissa and I began to hang out at the diner where Icky and Marilyn worked. They had an open mike every Friday night. Lissa's mother had to talk a blue streak to convince Rupert and Ruby that it was okay for me to go. We were the youngest there, since it was mainly a high school crowd. Lissa's mom told Ruby it would be educational. That's what won her over. She also promised to pick us up and drive me home. Silly, really, since I lived walking distance from the place. But those were the conditions. Rupert even said that I could stay out beyond my eight o'clock curfew, since the open mike didn't begin until nine.

Lissa and I had been coming for about three weeks when I decided to bring something to read. But it was hard to find the nerve to go up to the mike. That night we'd heard a poem about food, a poem about fat, and one about sex and politics. The puny poem that I'd brought couldn't compete. Compared to the fast talkers up at the mike, I might as well have not had a tongue.

"When are you going to read?" Lissa kept nagging. I'd ordered a burger from Icky at the grill, and she'd ordered a tomato and cheddar cheese sandwich. That was in the days before she went vegan.

"I changed my mind. I'm not going to read."

"You have to!" She was practically yelling. Icky glanced at me from the grill.

"Put your name on the list, kiddo. Let's hear what you've got."

"I can't. My poem isn't memorized."

"I'm signing up for you," Lissa said, hopping off of her seat.

"Don't worry, honey," Marilyn murmured, placing the burger in front of me. "These big kids won't bite you."

I was sweating. If you've ever done open mike, you know it's kind of like free fall. I was terrified—dry mouth, shaking legs, the whole bit. But when they called my name out, I somehow made it up there. My poem was in my pocket on a crumpled piece of paper. When I spoke into the mike, it started to squeak;

come to think of it, maybe it was my voice that was squeaking.

> *I have a friend*
> *Who likes to paint*
> *Works of nature*
> *Very quaint*
> *A leaf she spied upon the ground*
> *Became a fern-like lacy gown*
> *If I were naked, my request*
> *Would be that leaf upon my breast*
> *Tattooed, like an elf I'd dance*
> *Until discovered just by chance*

When I was finished, there was actually applause. I looked over at Lissa; she was beaming. Icky reached across and shook my hand when I got back to the counter.

"Good job, kiddo."

"Thanks."

I grabbed Lissa's hand. "Let's get out of here."

"Are you okay?" she asked, once we were outside.

"I guess. I didn't get booed anyway."

"You sounded great. I can't believe that your poem was about my painting."

"Why not?"

"It's just a silly little painting, Orphea."

"Well, it was just a silly little poem."

"My mom won't be here for another ten minutes," she said. "Want to go back inside?"

"No, let's wait out here." It was a chilly fall night, but there was a silver moon in the sky. We sat down on the sidewalk, leaning our backs against the outside wall of the diner.

"Look what I've got for us," Lissa whispered, digging into the pocket of her jacket and producing a lighter.

"What's that for?"

She reached into her other pocket and pulled out a half-smoked cigarette.

I felt a twinge of jealousy. Lissa was so square, but somehow she always seemed to be a few steps ahead of me.

"Wow, when did you pick that up?"

She grinned. "Yesterday. I found it in my sister's dresser drawer. I only smoked half and saved the rest for us."

She lit up and took a puff, then passed it over. I inhaled too deeply and coughed.

"I'm not sure I could get into it."

"Me either," she said, taking a drag. "But I figure, if you don't try something once, how can you give it up?"

"I guess . . ."

The wind began to rise. We huddled closer. . . .

■　■　■

She had gray eyes, gray the color of a cliff or gray the color of an ocean in a storm, depending on what mood she was in. People were always staring at her;

her face was a gorgeous puzzle. She was adopted, mixed with Korean and something else that she couldn't quite figure out.

"My birth mother didn't know my birth father's history," she told me. "She just knew that he was half Korean. So, I could be mixed with practically anything. My dad says who cares what the recipe is, just bottle it." Her gray eyes lit up. Lissa's dad adored her. I could barely remember my dad. Of course Nadine loomed large. Those big kisses, those swooping hugs. Ruby couldn't compete. Swooping a kid up into her arms just wasn't her style. To give her credit, she tried hard to take care of me. The meals she made were painstaking, a real labor of love considering that on most evenings she went to some kind of class, and that she ate so little herself. But when I ate with her before Rupert came home, I always felt like I was ruining something. I have terrible table manners—I slurp.

Anybody in the audience a slurper?

Well, you know what I mean; it's a way of eating that once you start you just can't break. Probably because it makes eating more fun. I find that if I make a little noise when I eat, the food tastes better.

When Ruby ate, she was silent. You couldn't even hear her chewing. Needless to say we weren't the ideal match at the supper table. There she'd sit carefully nibbling some curry or other that she'd spent at least an hour on, while I uncontrollably slurped. She flinched with my every forkful. When we had soup, things really got bad.

"Orphea, please make less noise. This isn't a barn-yard."

Or else she'd say something less direct like: "What are little girls made of?"

That was my cue to close my mouth when I chewed.

"Sugar and spice and everything nice," she'd answer for me.

I'd stop slurping and take very small sips of my soup. That's what "everything nice" meant—small sips. But it was no use; two minutes later, I'd slurp. She was such a good cook, all I could think of was tasting. Forget the manners.

Pretty soon, Ruby didn't sit down with me. She waited to eat something quick with Rupert. So unless I was at Lissa's, I dined alone, slurping everything from French toast to mashed potatoes.

My table manners were only one of the things about me that Ruby found irritating. You can't blame her, I guess. She didn't ask to be my new mother.

Lissa's parents, on the other hand, had picked her out. She was adopted. And she was an expert at doing just the right thing. Her mom would order outfits for her out of clothes catalogs without even asking Lissa's opinion—some ghastly checked shorts ensemble, for instance—and Lissa would *oooh* and *ahh* as if she adored it. Then she'd actually put the thing on and wear it to school.

"Why don't you ask your mom to let you pick out your own clothes?"

"That would ruin her fun."

"What about your fun? That outfit is geeky."

"Who cares?" That was courageous, believe me. In the place we went to school, people were scrutinized down to the toenail. If you lacked the right handbag, you could be ostracized; forget about growing your armpits, which is something I was secretly into. But Lissa would wear these Mom-picked outfits and hold her head high. The funny thing is that she could pull it off, because she was so gorgeous. But in her entire sixteen years, Lissa never once said no to her parents, about anything. I know that for a fact. Could be because of Annie, her older sister. Annie was her mom and dad's biological child. At the age of fifteen, she stole one of the family televisions to pawn for a bus ticket. The police had to bring her back. Lissa told me about a fight at dinner one evening, when her sister threw a fork at their dad and nearly put his eye out. Shortly after that, Annie ran away again, leaving behind all her stuff, and that time she didn't come back. . . . So, Lissa had to be the good one. But don't get me wrong—she was still her own person. She just managed to say yes to her parents about everything while doing precisely what she wanted to at the same time. She had a snake tattooed on her ankle that they never even knew about. I don't know how she hid it; she must have worn socks at the lake when she went swimming. When she got the tattoo, I went with her. The guy at the tattoo parlor asked for ID and Lissa gave them an old one that had belonged to Annie. Somehow it worked.

In high school, Lissa's paintings changed. She got into flowers, massive, fleshy flowers in psychedelic colors. A three-foot-high sunflower of hers won first place in the school art competition. The art teacher told Lissa that the painting was like Van Gogh. Lissa smiled politely when she heard that, but she wasn't pleased.

"I want to be like Georgia O'Keeffe," she said. "Lascivious." No mention of Picasso. I'll never forget a rose that she did—huge and velvety. But my favorite will always be the leaf she painted for me when we were twelve.

■ ■ ■

Let me take a breath.

After she peeled away in the van, I kept myself barricaded inside. I lost track of time. Three hours might have passed. I stayed huddled on the floor in front of my dresser, hunkered down for the next attack. I was scared to go downstairs. I didn't know what to do. Then the phone rang. I held my breath. I was sure it was Lissa on the line. She would have been worried about me; probably afraid that Rupert had killed me. Ruby had tried to protect me. Maybe if she answered she'd call me to the phone. But she didn't.

After that, silence. Or rather what I heard was a lack of noise, as if I were in the center of a vacuum. I hugged my knees and buried my head. The blood I'd tasted earlier had been coming from the side of my eye.

When Rupert had struck me, I'd been cut somehow, maybe by his wedding ring.

I wanted Nadine so much in that moment. I wanted her to pick up my whole room with me in it and toss it out of the window onto a gliding cloud that would take me and Lissa straight to a different world where it was no big deal for girls to French kiss. A world where people would let each other be who they are and mind their own business and concentrate on doing kind deeds or making poems and paintings or finding a cure for brain hemorrhages.

Finally, I stood up and began pushing the furniture away from my door. My mouth was dry as cotton and my legs were shaking. I had to call Lissa. One of the many weird features of life with Rupert and Ruby was that there was no phone above the first floor. And I wasn't permitted a cell phone. If I couldn't get to the phone downstairs, I decided, I'd go to Lissa's house instead. If Rupert tried to stop me, I'd fight my way out.

I picked up a shoe. If Rupert made a move to touch me again, I vowed to whack him in his teeth. That man loved his teeth. I pushed the bed away and cracked the door open. Rupert and Ruby were climbing the stairs.

"Come out, Orphea," my brother said. He sounded more grim than angry. He even sounded a little sorry.

"Don't be afraid," said Ruby. "Nobody's going to hurt you."

"You'd better not. I'll call the police!"

Rupert pushed the door open the rest of the way. They stood facing me.

"Move!" I tried to brush past them.

Rupert stopped me. "Don't go to Lissa's."

"I'll go where I please. Get out of my way."

"We have something to tell you," Ruby said timidly. She peered at my face. "Your poor eye . . ."

"Yeah! And who did that?"

Rupert cleared his throat. "I lost my temper."

"I'll say."

Ruby stepped closer. "Lissa's father just phoned."

"I hope she told him what Rupert did."

"I don't think so. You see, something bad happened."

"What could be worse than being beat almost senseless by your own brother?"

"Shut up and listen," snapped Rupert.

"Say what you have to say and let me out of here!"

Ruby touched my arm. "Lissa's spleen was ruptured."

"Her spleen?"

"The van skidded. An ambulance came—"

I felt a sick feeling inside. "Is she in the hospital? I have to see her."

"You can't. She's dead."

You made a portrait for my wall
Green
The inside of a leaf was all
Green
You wrapped me in a rainbow, girl
There was no springtime in my world
Until that green
Too new to pay the price
Our love became a vice
Sticks and stones may break my bones
Yet into the prism of your eye, I climb
To be a color so divine
To be your leaf
Green

UNACCEPTABLE

Dead?

Put yourself in my place—
No way—
I screamed in Rupert's face.
"Fuck you! Liar!"
"No need—"
"You're making it up!"
"Her father—"
"Fuck you!"

Ruby ran across the room with her hands over her
ears. "That filthy word!"

" 'Fuck you' is a phrase, you mouse-eyed no-mother.

A paper bag you could punch through. It's not a belt, not a whip, not your husband's fist that landed in my face. It's a phrase! So, fuck you!"

Rupert grabbed me by the collar and slapped me.

"I wanted to give you the benefit of the doubt, but now I see that you are incorrigible. Your friend just died and you're cursing at your mother."

"My friend didn't die! She's not my mother!"

"We don't have your kind of people in our family. Thank your lucky stars that we're willing to forgive you."

"Forgive me!"

"To forget what I saw. It's unacceptable! But I'm willing to forget, now that she's dead."

"Stop saying that! You asshole! I hate you!"

"Calm down, Orphea," Ruby said. "We're trying to be understanding. Lissa is—"

"I don't believe you!"

"Time out, Miss Tough-guy. Don't you scream at Ruby again! You and your friend acted like sluts. Don't think I didn't tell her—"

"What did you tell her?"

"Not to come back! Now, I'm sorry she died, but that's not my fault. And it doesn't give you the right—"

I fell on my knees and began to cry. Then, without warning, I threw up.

Rupert jumped out of the way. Ruby brought me a towel. I cleaned my face. I felt like the towel, soaked with vomit.

"Where is she?"

"Open Arms, I suppose," said Ruby. She looked worried. She was standing over me. Her voice sounded like an echo chamber. "Her folks will let us know the details. Want me to put something on your eye?"

"Don't—"

Rupert knelt down beside me. "What happened today is between these four walls." He leaned closer. "You don't have to worry. Hear me?"

What was he talking about?

He stood up. "Now get a grip on yourself."

They left me standing in the middle of my room. It was as if I were alone in the universe and the only center I had to hold on to was myself. And myself was petrified. Terrified. I wasn't crying anymore. I was waiting, while a tape inside my head kept saying that it couldn't be true; that Rupert and Ruby had made the whole thing up, which was incredibly vicious even for them. How could she be dead, when only this morning I had felt her breath on the back of my neck?

I opened my mouth and screamed. And I was sobbing into the quilt and pillow, seeing her face, drawing in ragged breaths of her fragrance, lemons, peanut butter, patchouli. My cheek fell upon a hard thing in the sheets, one of her earrings, a small gold hoop with an orange stone. I'm wearing it in my ear tonight, see? One of her striped socks appeared at the foot of the mattress. I cried until my sobs came up in dry heaves.

Suddenly my arms and legs began to move without me, as I threw on more clothes, a sweatshirt, my pink scarf, my red bandana, jeans. The T-shirt I had been sleeping in was torn and covered with dry blood. I ripped it off my body. I thrashed across the room, crazily getting ready—for what? Only my arms and legs knew, and my hands, which deftly creased the red bandana and laid it across my forehead above the cut on my eye, and quickly made a knot at the back of my head, above the nape of my neck. Why was I getting dressed up? Was I dressed up? I opened the door to my room and raced down the stairs, heedless of falling, not anticipating in my mind the number of steps in my stride. Almost as if I were flying, down and onto the carpet and out the wooden door. Then I was slipping on the sidewalk. My sneakers were soaked and I'd forgotten my own socks, though I had Lissa's in my pocket.

Where am I going? My thoughts rambled. What just happened? This can't be real.

But my feet knew where to go. They led me slipping through ten blocks of slush to Open Arms Funeral Home.

■ ■ ■

I will find you
Pebble in the snow
Needle hid in hay
Trembling drop in ocean's spray
My feet will take me
I will touch you with frozen toes
Pricked finger
With parched tongue I will drink you
You are my sole elixir

■ ■ ■

SUNFLOWER

When I got to Open Arms, a lamp was burning in the window. There was no sign of Lissa's parents. The door was unlocked. A statue of an angel hovered over the lobby. The place was like a velvet womb, red velvet drapes, red velvet chairs. My arms were yearning to hold Lissa. Somewhere, I was hoping that she wasn't dead.

I tiptoed across the lobby and began wandering the corridors—not a soul in sight. But I heard someone humming a scratchy, nondescript tune. A door at the end of the corridor was partway open. The humming was coming from there. I walked to the door and slipped inside the room. A small woman with gray hair was stooped over an open coffin.

My legs buckled. The air was filled with the strong smell of chemicals. The woman turned around and glanced up at me. She wore thick glasses. In her hand was a small paintbrush. What could she possibly be painting?

"Are you all right, dear?" Her face was soft as dough.

"My friend . . ."

The woman stood up and motioned toward the coffin. "Are you the granddaughter? They told me that you might come."

Totally confused at this point, I felt a thick lump rose in my throat. "Is that Lissa?"

"Lissa? No, this is Virginia." She stepped away from the coffin to permit me a view.

I took a few steps forward and saw the face of an elderly woman, carefully powdered and rouged. Her top lip had lipstick; the bottom lip was pale. I sighed with relief.

"We're not quite ready yet," the attendant explained. I glanced again at the tiny brush and understood. She was the makeup artist.

"So Lissa Evans isn't here? She's not dead?"

The woman led me to a stool.

"She's my friend. She's only sixteen. Someone told me she died. It could be a mistake."

"We're expecting an Evans," she said quietly.

I felt a stab of pain. "Are you sure?"

"I don't have the details. Is there someone that I can call for you? Someone to drive you home?"

"No." I stood up and peeked at the corpse. "Somebody's grandma?"

"Ninety-five. Died at a party."

A tear rolled down my cheek.

"Lissa never wore makeup. She wouldn't like lipstick."

"Don't worry, I'll take good care of her. I'll tell her you stopped by. . . ."

■ ■ ■

After that I went to Icky's. The diner had closed early on account of the weather. I knocked and Marilyn let me in. When I tried to explain what had happened, she and Icky didn't understand at first.

"Were you driving?"

"I wasn't in the car."

"Then how were you in the accident?"

"I wasn't."

"You're still in shock. She's in shock, Icky. She must have been in the accident—look at her."

They were confused by my cuts and bruises. And I guess I *was* in a state of shock.

"Lissa was driving. She was leaving my house. She was alone."

"Is she okay?" That was Marilyn.

"Her spleen broke."

Icky cracked his knuckles. "Poor girl. Where'd you get that fat lip, then?"

I lowered my eyes. "Rupert was mad at us."

"Your brother did that?"

I began sobbing. "Don't worry about me. Lissa is the one. Her spleen . . ."

"Where is she?" asked Marilyn. "In the hospital?"

"I went to see her body, but she wasn't there."

Icky's face turned into itself, but Marilyn kind of exploded.

"Her body? Oh dear Lord, no! Oh, Orphea. Oh, Lissa." She hugged me and the two of us were crying and Icky was pacing.

"Did that jerk brother of yours do something to cause Lissa to wreck?"

"She was by herself. It just happened. I haven't talked to her parents. But I can't tell them what was going on, anyway, because they don't know."

"Know what?" Marilyn asked.

"Lissa and I, well, we were making out." I glanced away. "I don't know what you think about something like that. We'd just figured out . . . our feelings . . . and then Rupert came into my room and Lissa ran out and . . ."

Icky put a hand on my shoulder. "You don't have to explain your private stuff to us. I can't believe your brother would give you a fat lip over something like that. I mean, he could have his opinions . . ."

"I'd better go. Lissa's family might be calling. The whole thing might be a mistake. There isn't a body."

"Whoa—you're not going yet. Marilyn is going to see to your face. When's the last time you ate something?" He clenched his fist. "That brother of yours is some coward, beating up on children."

Marilyn gave me some ice for my lip and cleaned the cut on my eye. I put on a pair of her socks. Icky made me sunny-side up eggs with jelly and toast. I stared at the plate.

"Sunflowers."

"What is it, hon?" That was Marilyn.

"Sunflowers." The egg yolks were bright yellow orbs. "If you stare long enough, the eggs turn into sunflowers. Don't you see them?"

"It's going to be okay, honey." Icky was speaking. "Hold on."

"I don't know if I can." My mind was a splitting fissure. I felt like I might fall in.

"Eat your sunflowers, kiddo. Come on."

I couldn't.

"I don't want you to go back," said Marilyn as I got up to leave. "Your brother might hurt you again."

"He won't. . . ."

Rupert and Ruby didn't like slurping or unpolished shoes, wrinkled jeans, loud radios, ringing telephones, or the way I held my cup; but that was the first time I'd been hit. They went to school for parent conferences. They had money for me to go to college. After all those years, Ruby still tried giving me hugs.

But she never asked what I was thinking. They

couldn't guess how unfinished I felt. They never came to hear me read my poetry.

Seeing Lissa and me together must have been shocking. But they still loved me in their own way. Didn't they?

"My brother won't hit me again."

"Stay here with us," Icky pleaded.

"No, I should go."

So Icky walked me home and gave me his cell number. "Call me if you have trouble. I'll stand outside the house. I won't leave until you wave."

Rupert and Ruby were already in bed, or at least they were in their bedroom. I paused at the phone in the hallway and listened to my messages. My heart thumped. There was one from Mr. Evans, who sounded like he was having trouble breathing.

"Hi, Orphea. Ahh . . . I've spoken to your brother, so I know that you've gotten the news. I'm wondering, ahh . . . she was a good little driver . . . it was the snow, I suppose. I had just checked the car. . . . We're still in a state of shock. . . . We're having a memorial service at the boathouse next to the lake. Day after tomorrow. Asking that her friends bring something to say about her. No pressure. Ahh . . .

"But you were her best friend.

"One of us will call with more details tomorrow. Bye."

I went to the window and waved.

■ ■ ■

I stayed in my room until the funeral, surviving on a bag of marshmallows and water from the bathroom. Ruby and Rupert let me be. The only way I can describe how I felt is "cotton candy." Like a big, sticky ball filled with air. My body was a wad of nothing about to vanish. But my brain was going overtime. I wanted to say something at the service. Something significant. I scrawled disjointed ideas in my journal—

Lissa was a kind person . . . always thinking of others. . . .

We planned a road trip for after high school.

New York, L.A., Grand Canyon, both oceans . . .

But the first stop, she said, was for me. Proud Road.

Dinky town not on the map where I always wanted to go.

"If it's important to you, Orphea, we'll go."

That was Lissa.

I didn't think we could do it. She said we'd save our money. Get a car. Drive off and not look back.

"It's your movie, Orphea," she said. "You might as well write the script."

What she didn't know was that I didn't have a movie, not of my own. I was just a part of hers, because she was the dreamer.

Being in Lissa's movie . . . the best part of my life so far.

I didn't get to see Lissa at the service. Her family had her cremated. The boathouse was packed with kids from school, especially from the literary magazine, where Lissa did art and I did poetry. A guy we both knew from grade school named Mike came over and put his arm around me.

"How you doing, sweetheart? Y'all were always so tight."

"Okay, Mike."

He gave me a curious look. I was wearing shades, but my face was still puffy.

"You sure?"

"Yep."

He shook his head. "We're all going to miss her."

Lissa's dad told the story of how when Lissa had been four years old she'd jumped off the dock at the lake without her water wings, even though she didn't know how to swim. She'd gotten this idea that on the morning of her fourth birthday, she'd be able to swim just like that. And she'd tried it. But Mr. Evans had to fish her out. She had a magic way of thinking sometimes, he said, and she wasn't afraid to take risks.

Mrs. Evans didn't say anything. Lissa's sister, Annie, wasn't there.

At one point Mr. Evans gave me a nod, but I pretended not to notice. At the last minute, I had decided not to speak after all. My feelings were like a dammed-up waterfall. I wasn't sure what would happen if I opened my mouth. After the service, when Mrs. Evans gave me a hug, my body was stiff as cardboard, I was trying so hard to hold back. They were her parents. They were being so brave. It wasn't my place to make a scene.

"You were her best friend," her dad whispered into my ear.

I loved her! I wanted to shout it to the world. But I kept quiet. Instead, in a sealed envelope next to the urn, I left a poem. God took her for a reason—that's what the minister said. I didn't believe that. Death had taken Lissa. And Death is a whole 'nother being.

I was the kite
You were my rescue
I was a whisper
You were my ear
You are the flower on my altar
I have no voice unless you hear
No ear
No voice
No rescue
I stand waiting
For you to appear

CRAZY

So, folks . . .

I see Marilyn coming around if you need to place
an order. I recommend today's special. Whoops!—Icky
just put a spot on her—whoa, that's bright. . . . Bring
it down some, Icky. Okay? Great, that's better. . . . I'll
just take a sip of water myself. . . .

So, where were we?

Lissa's death left me in a dark place.

■ ■ ■

I lasted in school for about three weeks, pretending to be there when I wasn't. I disappeared, burrowing into her absence. In the hallway, people smiled at me kindly. I responded with a mechanical upward tilt of my mouth. Best friends, they were all thinking; tied at the waist; more than friends, some might have guessed. I spoke only when necessary. The world took on sadness so profound that even taste buds were affected. One afternoon I made a smoothie in the blender, something that Lissa and I used to do; fresh strawberries, bananas, ice, milk, vanilla, and that day an overripe mango—I still have the image of my thumbnail pushing the skin away from fleshy fruit. Then it was all in the blender whirring away. I took a taste and where there should have been sweetness on my tongue, there was just the taste of sad. I went upstairs to the bathroom and shaved my head, which gave Ruby yet another complaint and so made me not only sad but foolish. Since I was a fool, one night I carved that onto my skin, using a safety pin, delicately scratching the letter F and all the other letters onto my forearm. Not that I actually believed that I was a fool. That was just an excuse. Scratching my arm with the pin was an exit, you see, a way to let the pain out. But the exit wasn't big enough. If I scratched the whole alphabet into my flesh I could never let it all out, the pain I was feeling inside. Ordinarily I would have written in my journal instead of on my arm, but writing was a thing I'd done in my other life, the life I had with Lissa.

Have any of you experienced that kind of loss? There you are living a little peanut-butter-and-jelly-type existence, surviving school, answering e-mail, seeing a flick, counting the days until your escape from the dry prison walls of high school and the ruthless eye of the sadist who calls himself your guardian, and BINGO! Fate trips you up, cracks open your chest, yanks out your heart, cuts it in half with a sharp pair of scissors, and then stuffs it back inside of you. And the world tells you to keep on going. Got to keep reading those books, if you want to get into a decent college. Got to write those papers. When Lissa died, I was in the middle of *Moby-Dick*. Why would I want to read about a whale at a time like that? Even if I were interested, there was no way I could fit all those words into my mind. My mind was filled with images. Images of her, like photographs stuffed into a drawer so full that it could no longer move. A stuck drawer, stuffed with pictures of our lives completely out of order, chaotic, careening clips of our own private movie. How could I think about precalc when I was feeling like that?

After sad and foolish came crazy. I ransacked Ruby's medicine cabinet, took some pills and chased them with vodka, but found myself still standing. So, I took a walk to Icky's diner and put in an order for my very last supper, BLT on a sesame roll. The soup of the day was split pea. To this day, I'm not sure whether it was the pills and vodka or the smell of the simmering kettle that sent me flying to the bathroom. Marilyn held my head over the toilet.

"What did you take? Tell me what you took!"

"Some kind of pills so Ruby could get pregnant," I said, gagging.

She slammed me on the back. "They probably won't kill you."

But by the time I was done being sick, I felt like a ghost. I curled up on the floor of the diner's kitchen while Icky lectured me.

"You don't do that kind of stuff, hear me? You don't take your own precious life. That's not your place to do that, Orphea. Your job is to—"

"To live," said Marilyn.

"You ain't the only one who's ever lost somebody they love." Icky's voice rained down on me. I closed my eyes. I wanted to follow her.

"You think that Lissa would want this bullshit? You think that she would approve?"

They didn't understand. They hadn't been there. Maybe Lissa wanted to die after what had happened. Maybe she couldn't deal with it.

"Lissa was so bubbly and very wise," Marilyn said. "She would never, ever do something like try to kill herself. That was not Lissa."

How did they know? How could anyone know what she felt when Rupert went downstairs to rub her nose in it? He had seen us. She would have felt ashamed. She would have been afraid of him calling her parents. Maybe she wrecked the van on purpose. . . .

■ ■ ■

A few days later, I was back at the diner. I'd been avoiding the open-mike nights, but Icky's coffee had become my regular diet. After closing, he and Marilyn invited me upstairs to their apartment. They had something to tell me. Seemed they were leaving town; they'd been planning it for quite a while but I hadn't known. The news came as a blow. Now that Lissa was gone, they were the only people in the world who understood what I was going through. Oh, Mrs. Evans had called once or twice since the memorial, but there was a distance between us; I'm sure it was because I couldn't be honest about all that had happened the morning of the accident. How could I? Lissa might not have wanted them to know. Who was I to spoil the memory of their perfect girl? But Icky and Marilyn knew everything. And now they were leaving.

"Where are you going? Why?"

"We got our own place." Marilyn sounded so happy.

"She saw it in the tea leaves," bragged Icky.

"But you have your own place. You work here. You're the boss."

"The diner is okay, but we don't own it."

"Besides, we don't want a diner. We want a club. And now we got a club in Queens, New York!"

"Queens, New York? What's wrong with Pennsylvania?"

"I got a grandma in Queens," said Marilyn.

"We've been living in Pennsylvania for long enough," said Icky. "We would have left a few years ago, if it wasn't for my parole."

"Parole?"

"Been a long road to here from juvie," he said, sheepishly. "Used to be a young arsonist. Mind you, not something I'm proud of, but I paid my debt. Now we're going to have our dream, our own little club. Right, Marilyn?"

Marilyn snuggled up. "Yes, Icarus, dear. In the Big Apple. Just like I saw in the tea leaves."

"Who cares about some old dumb tea leaves? You can have your own club right here!"

"We already got the spot. We put down the deposit," said Icky. "This is our dream."

"It'll be paradise," said Marilyn. "We'll serve coffee and have a juice bar. All the poets and artists will come. Icky's going to have theatrical lights! I'll play bass!"

My eyes stung with tears.

"Great, guys. Congratulations."

Marilyn touched my shoulder. "This summer we're hoping you'll visit us."

"You mean it?"

"You can't get rid of us that easy," said Icky.

"So will you come?" asked Marilyn.

"Yeah, if Rupert and Ruby let me."

They exchanged glances. Marilyn went into the bedroom. She brought back an envelope.

"Take this."

"What's in it?"

"Two hundred bucks. We thought you might need a loan. Use it if you need to get out in a hurry. Get my drift?"

Icky laid a hand on my head. My hair had barely begun growing out. "We don't like leaving you with that brother of yours."

"Thanks. But I can't take the money."

"Sure you can."

"It's too much. I can't pay it back."

Icky smiled. "We don't want the money. Pay us back in poems."

"You must be joking. I don't even write anymore."

"You will," said Marilyn.

"But two hundred dollars . . . I'd have to write four hundred poems to pay you back."

"How about twenty?" said Icky.

I managed a smile. "Lissa wouldn't believe this. When we were in junior high I used to sell my poems in the grocery store parking lot, while Lissa played the guitar—"

"I didn't know she played guitar," said Marilyn.

"She didn't. She was horrible. But it got people's attention, so I'd get to sell a few poems. Then we'd split the proceeds for pizza."

"How much were you charging then?"

"Fifty cents."

"See there—your price has gone up! One day you'll be rich and famous."

"Does it say so in the tea leaves?" I joked.

"Not yet. But one thing I know for sure is that someday we'll be together. . . . "

A lump rose in my throat. "When are you leaving?"

"A few days from now."

"You have our cell number," said Icky, "but we'll call you before we go."

Marilyn hugged me. "No more pills, promise?"

"Promise."

Icky shook my hand. "You owe us poems, kiddo. Don't stiff us."

I didn't know it at the time, but I'd be leaving town before they did.

Everybody has got a story to tell
Everybody has got an eye
The truth is what you want to see
In your body's mind
Your mind and mine clicked like gold
You whispered that my hand was old
The lifeline long though fractured at the palm
Was it this hurt that you foretold?
You with your soul of an ancient seer
Next to my thumb did you glimpse the slippery road?
Or was it my future you felt when I held your hand in
    mine
My bitch friend Fate, dying to get on a roll
Still, I am yours, embraced by time
Those moments when we touched enshrined
Forever in my body's mind

FOOTSTEPS

Any jet-setters in the crowd? Once I went to Kenya. . . .

But I went before I was born, so you may not think that counts. Nadine and Daddy went on their honeymoon and Nadine was already pregnant. So I was there, on board in her stomach so to speak. Nadine told me about it. She told me that when she was on the hotel balcony, she pulled up her shirt while no one was looking so that her belly was bare. Since I couldn't see any of Kenya, she wanted me to at least feel the heat of the sun through her skin. I don't remember that either, of course, but Nadine assured me that I felt it.

The only other trip I took was to the mountains in Virginia, to a town called Handsome Crossing. Nadine had grown up there in a place called Proud Road. Proud Road, named for my family. I was around three when that happened. Nadine had been incredibly attached to her family. So much so that she wanted me to have their last name. She insisted on it with Daddy and got her way. So, my name got to be Proud like Nadine's. Rupert was Jones like Daddy. Rupert wouldn't have been a Proud at any rate, since we had different mothers. I never knew a thing about Rupert's mother except that she moved to Cleveland. She came from Handsome Crossing, too, and she hated Nadine on account of how Nadine had stolen her husband. If you're wondering how I know that, Nadine told me. Weird, how she confided in a small child. Or maybe not weird. Daddy was a lot older. When I was born, she was just seventeen. Seventeen, same age I am now.

When Nadine died, Rupert wanted my name changed to Jones since he and Ruby would be my guardians. When I found out, I went on a hunger strike. I was already so sad in my gray world. Why eat a gray piece of broccoli? A mysterious hand had snatched my mother away. Nobody was taking my name. I'd starve first. Luckily, Ruby took pity on me.

"Look at her Rupert, she's so pathetic," Ruby would say. "You don't need another girl named Jones, as long as you've got me."

"She'll be Jones as long as she lives in my house." His house? My house, you mean! It's where I'd lived my whole life! That house belongs to us both! But Rupert thinks it belongs to him more, because Nadine made him the executor. Well, he may have been in charge of the house, but he was not in charge of my name!

"You're Orphea Jones," he would argue.

"Orphea Proud," I would say stubbornly.

"Orphea Jones!" he would shout. "Eat those peas!"

"I hate peas, you jackass!"

"Did you hear that, Ruby? Go wash her mouth out with soap."

I would trot off with Ruby to the bathroom, leaving my peas on the plate.

"Why do you anger him so?" Ruby would sigh.

"He hates me. Anyway, I'm Orphea Proud."

"He doesn't hate you," Ruby would say, washing my face. She never, ever washed out my mouth. "Brothers and sisters always fight. Besides, he's under pressure. Dental school is harder than he thought."

I scowled. "Orphea Proud."

"Okay, Miss Proud," Ruby would say. "I'll see what I can do." Then she'd start to make a little braid in my hair. Ruby's braids hurt. They were too tight. I liked the way Nadine braided.

"Stop wiggling, Miss Sugar 'n' Spice."

Sugar 'n' spice? Maybe lemon and hot sauce or better still turpentine and Worcestershire. Never sugar and spice, though. But I have to hand it to Ruby. Thanks to her, I kept my name. It was one of the only things I had left to remind me of Nadine. I also had the wall hanging, which she had brought home from Kenya. It was one of the first things I showed Lissa when she came over. I also showed her the picture of me and Nadine when we were on Proud Road when I was three. Lissa never got tired of looking at it with me. That's the kind of friend she was. She never got tired of hearing me tell the same story over and over.

"It had a nice smell." She was listening to me again. She was holding the picture, looking at every detail as if for the first time.

"What did it smell like?"

"Woodsmoke." I took a little sniff, trying to imagine. "Woodsmoke mixed with snow clouds."

"That's because you were there in winter," she said, pressing the picture to her nose. "You were there when it was snowing." She held the picture up to the light. "Your mom is so pretty."

"Thanks."

"And you're so weird-looking."

"Thanks again, I guess."

"Your feet, they're so big!"

"I was wearing someone's snow boots. How many times do I have to tell you?"

"Duckfeet!"

"Stop it," I whined.

"I like your mittens, though. I can hardly see what color they were, the picture is so faded. What color were they again?"

"Red. And my mom's coat is brown. I'll never forget her coat. I used to bury my nose in it."

"Oh, Orphea, I'm sorry."

"It's okay. I'm not sad anymore. I just wish I could go there again."

"Do you think it's changed?"

"How could it be the same if Nadine isn't there?"

"What about the aunts?"

"I don't know them. They just send me a card every Christmas with a dollar bill in it."

She winced. "Do you think they're poor?"

"Who knows?"

We put our heads together and stared at the photo. It was covered with my thumbprints. My mom and I both had round dark eyes. Clouds of breath floated in front of our faces.

"Looks cold there," said Lissa.

"It was cold the time I was there."

"What about the other time?"

"What other time?"

She stared at the ceiling. She was talking about Nadine's funeral. I'd told her how I'd thrown myself on the coffin.

"It was springtime then."

"Hey! I see something! Did you ever see this?"

"In the picture? What?"

"There!" she said, plopping down on the bed. "Footsteps!" She pointed to a spot with her pinky. "Footsteps in the snow! They must be yours. That's so cute!"

I grabbed the picture. "Let's see." I squinted, trying to see what she had seen. She leaned over and pointed to a tiny trail of specks.

"Are you sure that's not dirt?"

"They're footsteps. Don't you see?"

I shrugged. "Amazing. All these years I've had the picture and I never knew they were there."

She poked me in the ribs. "Because you really weren't looking, Duckfeet."

"Oh my gosh—I just had a memory!"

"Something new?"

"Yes! I remember making my footsteps! I was making them with the boots that were too big for me. And I thought that my footsteps looked like a giant's. Like the giant's in *Jack and the Beanstalk*! I told Nadine and she started laughing at me and so did some other people."

"Maybe the aunts!"

"Yeah, maybe. That's so cool—I can remember the actual feeling . . . making a footstep in the snow. That was the first time I ever remember seeing snow."

"We should go there," Lissa said.

"Where?"

"Proud Road."

"When? It's miles and miles away."

"We'll make it a stop on our road trip."

"But you want to go to L.A. to find your birth mother."

"We'll stop on our way."

"Come on, Lissa. You don't have to go to some hick place on top of a mountain, just because I have a picture on my dresser."

"It probably isn't a hick place at all. It could be artistic!" *Artistic* was one of our favorite words in those days. "Anyway, you and Nadine are in the picture. I want to be there, too."

"Where?"

"With you on Proud Road . . ."

■ ■ ■

A couple of days after my visit with Icky and Marilyn, Rupert surprised me in the front hall when I got back from school. It was unheard of for him to be home at that hour. It was even early for me, but since Lissa died I'd been skipping out on after-school activities. Rupert had a drink in his hand. Not that he ever overdid it; he never drank more than one, three ounces of bourbon over cracked ice with a pinch of sugar and a slice of lemon. Since he asked me to make it sometimes, I had the drink down pat.

"You're home early."

"I was waiting for you." Cutting right to the chase, he presented me with Icky's envelope. "Where'd you get this?"

"None of your business. Don't tell me you've been in my room?"

"I'm your guardian. If you're stealing, I need to know."

"You know I don't steal."

"How do I know that? I thought I knew you, but then—"

"If you're referring to me and Lissa, drop it. If you hadn't busted into my room that morning, she'd be alive. What were you doing? Listening at the ceiling for a squeak in the bed?"

"You had that ignorant music blaring. That's why I opened the door. I knocked but you didn't hear me."

"So now Lissa is dead." Inside I was boiling with red-hot anger. "Guess you wish I died, too."

"Oh, come off it."

"Then you wouldn't have to be reminded of the horrible, disgusting sight that you saw—two girls hugging, ooh!"

He put down his glass. "I saw a lot more than hugging."

"Yeah and you freaked out," I taunted. "You tried to kill me."

"Don't be so melodramatic."

"You busted my lip. You cut my eye. Icky and Marilyn saw me that day. That's why they gave me the two hundred dollars, to get away from you."

He snarled. "You got the money from that lowlife?"

"They're not lowlifes. They're good people. They're kind. Something you wouldn't know about."

"They wouldn't be so kind if they knew you were a slut."

"I'm not a slut! Give me my money."

"No."

"Come on, Rupert. It's a business deal. They're paying me to write poems."

"I'm supposed to believe that?"

"Believe what you like. Just don't take my money. You have enough of your own. You don't need mine."

He grabbed my shoulder. A shiver went through me.

"Let go of me. I have to do homework."

"You haven't done homework in weeks. Ruby spoke to your teachers. You're flunking out, and you used to be an A student. All because of some identity crisis."

"What are you talking about?"

"That thing with you and Lissa—Ruby read about it—two girls who don't know who they are, pretending to be boys. Some sick experiment."

"It wasn't like that!"

"Is that what your Icky and Marilyn friends say? I hear the guy's an ex-con and who knows what rock she crawled out from under."

"They understand me more than you ever did. And they know all about me and Lissa!"

His face darkened with rage. "You told them?"

"Yes."

"Are you trying to ruin me?"

"It has nothing to do with you."

He raised his hand. I moved out of the way.

"You'd better not hit me again!"

"I'll do better than that," he said, turning away. "You're grounded. Don't leave this house."

■　■　■

All that evening I was on pins and needles. Ruby came home and cooked; then she dragged Rupert off to tango class, of all the insane things. Even after she got her degree, Ruby was always studying something. I was relieved when I heard my brother's car roll out of the driveway. I thought of calling Marilyn and Icky, but I knew they'd be busy getting ready to leave. If only I were going with them . . .

The very next day after school, Rupert and Ruby met me at the door. My duffel bag and knapsack were in the front hall.

"What's that?"

"You're leaving," said Rupert.

"What?"

"You're out of control," Ruby said. She avoided my eyes.

"Fine. Where am I going?"

"That's for us to know and you to find out," Rupert taunted. "Get in the car."

"Not until I know where I'm going."

"Don't start."

"Just get in," Ruby pleaded. "It's for your own good."

"Can I at least go to my room, before you kick me out?"

"Five minutes," said Rupert.

I splashed some water onto my face in the bathroom. My closet was pretty cleaned out. I grabbed the picture of me and Nadine and my journal. I was excited but also terrified. Maybe they were sending me to a psycho ward, where doctors would think I was crazy and dope me all up. I tried to get a grip. Anywhere would be better than being with Rupert.

"Let's go."

"You seem eager," said Rupert.

"Nothing left here for me."

He hurled my stuff into the car, and the three of us took off.

■ ■ ■

The trip was endless. I still had no idea where I was headed. I'd acted tough in front of Rupert, but honestly I was scared shitless. Pretty soon it was dark. I occupied myself by floating on the ceiling. A kind of out-of-body experience thing that's really easy to do if you have imagination. Lissa is the one who taught me how to do it. First you close your eyes and imagine that you hear the buzzing of a fly. The buzzing noise tells you that the fly is hovering near. Next, you imagine that you see the fly; it's hovering right above the center of your head, never leaving that spot. It's only a hop and a skip to seeing yourself hovering up there with it. Then you experience a floating sensation and you're on your own. You're still sitting on the car seat, as in my case, but at the same time you're also hovering up near the ceiling, looking down. Having a view of yourself from above is liberating, especially if you can also imagine boring your way up through the roof of the car and getting outside. Then you're looking down not only at yourself, but at your car, the car in front and the one behind you, the landscape, and the highway. It's kind of like flying, no, actually, more like floating. Anyway, that's what I did.

That's only one of the tricks that Lissa taught me. She also taught me how to see people naked, and better still, in Rupert and Ruby's case, see them as skeletons. I got a kick out of that. There they were in the front seat; thinking that I was all subdued, when in fact I wasn't even in the car. I had escaped to the top of the world, where I could see them as they really were, a couple of skeletons. I found it very relaxing, so much so that I fell into a sleep where bits of me melted like sugar before I tumbled into blackness.

I dreamed of Lissa. She'd stayed over. It was the night before the snow day. A damp smell filled the air. I read her a new poem. We were sitting on the side of my bed. The poem was about a spider. It was peculiar, nothing like what I'd written before, this ditty that sounded kind of like a nursery rhyme. I recited in this screechy voice to make Lissa laugh. She doubled over onto the bed and kicked her legs up. We were so silly. She threw a pillow at me and I ducked. But I kept on reciting the poem. We were so happy. Suddenly in the dream there was a real spider on Lissa's forehead. Huge. She didn't know it was there. She was still laughing. Then I felt something on my thigh, and there was another spider, just as huge, on my leg. I opened my mouth to scream, but nothing came out. I looked over at Lissa again and *she* was a spider! And so was I! I woke up screaming at the top of my lungs, and Rupert and Ruby were shouting for me to shut up. But I kept right on, seeing how it was driving them crazy. Frankly I'm not sure I could have stopped. Something had snapped inside me.

I screamed myself hoarse, over the blaring radio, which Ruby had turned up to top volume to drown me out. Then Rupert pulled off onto the shoulder and got out. He threw a cold cup of coffee in my face. It stunned me but I still kept screaming. Screaming in rage, screaming in pain, screaming because I hated them and blamed them for what had happened.

Ruby got out, too. She opened my door and glared down at me. She looked possessed.

"Shut up!"

Then she did something really un-Ruby-like. She slid in beside me and got me in a headlock. Rupert got in the other side and gagged my mouth with her scarf. Then he bound my hands behind me with his necktie. It happened so fast. "Lie down," Ruby ordered. "You're overwrought."

No kidding!

"I'll stay back here with you," she said, pressing down on my back until my face was flat on the seat. "Get some sleep!"

I didn't sleep, but I did bite her expensive scarf. I also tried to tear my brother's expensive necktie.

Just before dawn, we stopped abruptly, the only car in sight on a winding dirt road. Outside, the moon and sun were trading places, making the sky a split screen between night and day.

Rupert opened the front door and then Ruby

opened mine. For a giddy moment, I imagined that they'd driven me to some Godforsaken place to murder me.

Ruby undid the gag and my seat belt. I lurched past her, slamming my feet onto the ground, my legs throbbing from sitting so long in the same position. Approaching me cautiously, Rupert untied my hands.

"We're here," he announced in a weary voice. He gestured up the hill with his head. "I can't take a chance of my car getting stuck. You'd think they'd get a decent road after all these years in this hillbilly place. Go on! You can walk the rest of the way."

I blinked, trying to orient myself. There didn't appear to be a single house.

"You can't leave me here," I said breathlessly. "Leave me somewhere else. Leave me in a city."

"This is where your mother's people are. Let them deal with you now."

"They're expecting you," said Ruby. "We didn't tell them about . . . you know . . . Lissa."

"And you'd better not, either," warned Rupert.

"What did you tell them?"

"That you had some problems in school and you need a break."

I smirked. "What kind of problems?"

"Make something up. And watch what you say. And mind your p's and q's. People down here are righteous."

"Righteous?"

"They do the right thing. And if you don't, they knock some sense in your head."

He jammed an envelope into my hand. "There's a check made out to your aunts for your expenses. That way nobody can say that I shirked my duty. The two hundred dollars from your lowlife friends is in there, too."

My heart hammered against my chest. He tossed my bags out onto the ground.

"Why do you hate me, Rupert?"

"Because you're ungrateful. You want to throw away what my father worked all his life to build."

"What are you talking about?"

"His reputation. He'd roll over in his grave if he knew what you'd become."

Ruby stepped up and gave me my journal. I handed her the scarf.

"Be good, Orphea. Forget those feelings you had about Lissa. You can start over here. . . ."

Then they got into the car.

"Where's the house?"

"Up the road and around the bend," Rupert called out. "They live in a store."

He turned the car around and headed back down the hill. Up ahead there was fog. I stood rooted to one spot. Everything was still. I started shaking inside.

I picked up my stuff and trudged up the road. My legs and arms were so tired, walking up the hill was like walking through waves. Then I saw a sign hanging off one of its nails. The chipped paint letters spelled out PROUD ROAD. I walked faster. My feet were suddenly freezing. Around the bend was a crooked house built behind a boulder. Like the sign, the building needed a paint job, but I could tell that it had once been bright pink. A second sign hung above its wraparound porch: PROUD STORE, MINERVA AND CLEOPATRA PROUD, PROPRIETORS. I climbed the stairs. Next to the door was a pile of wood and hanging at the windows were white lace curtains. I knocked, but no one answered. I opened the door to the tinkling of a bell. In the middle of the room was a potbellied stove with a fire going. I took a sniff and recognized that fragrance from long ago, woodsmoke mixed with snow clouds. By the stove there was a table with a checked cloth; straight ahead, an old-fashioned soda fountain with red leather stools; beyond that, a wall filled with faded photos and old license plates. And everywhere else there were shelves, mainly empty but here and there with cans or boxes.

A faint snore came from the left of the doorway. An old woman with her hair in gray coils sat slumped behind a low counter, her hands folded in front of the cash register, her shoulders covered with a quilt that looked like a map. I had missed her on my way in. Was she Aunt Minerva or Aunt Cleopatra? I stared, trying to recognize her face. But I couldn't. I turned and closed the front door quietly.

Suddenly a short, stocky creature in a gingham apron shot out of one of the side rooms.

"Hey there, Orphea, honey child!" she called out.

Her voice was low and gravelly. "Must not have heard the doorbell. We've been expecting you."

"Aunt Minerva?" I guessed.

"That's me."

She clomped across the room and gave me a bear hug. Then Aunt Cleo woke up.

"Oh my! Is she here?" Her voice was high and wispy. "Where's that bad boy, Rupert? Oh, never mind."

She scooted out from behind the counter still in her chair! A wheelchair—something else I hadn't remembered. She grabbed my arms and pulled me down to give me a kiss on the cheek.

"Welcome home. You must be hungry."

I sat down at the table in front of the stove. Aunt Minerva brought me hot fritters. My eyes began to close after one bite. Then I felt Aunt Cleo's hand patting my knee. . . .

Proud Road is another country. You'd probably think it's the middle of nowhere or even the end of the world. I think of it as the land of softness in honor of the quilts and pillows my two aunts gave me to take up to a loft, where I slept for a week.

The wind was harsh, but I recall
A curl of smoke, thread through my hair
On my mittens, on your coat
A curl of smoke, weaving air
Footsteps when I first saw snow
In my brain forever branded
Slain bough of an apple tree
Rock me sweetly up to heaven
Now I lay me, downy quilt

Intermission

I'm gonna take five, so I'll ask Marilyn Chin to come up and play the bass!

Icky Digits will come down and take your orders, soon as he turns the lights up.

If anybody wants to stretch their legs and get a closer look at Ray's masterpiece—which I'm not supposed to be looking at—be our guest. Right, Ray? How you doin' back there, anyway? Don't forget—more than one horse isn't allowed! Has Raynor Grimes been painting horses all this time? Don't tell me—he better not be. . . .

See you guys in a bit.

SECRETS

Do you have a secret? I won't ask you to tell, don't worry. I just want you to think about it for a moment.

There are all kinds of secrets, of course. Little secrets that rest in a corner of your mind, neatly as a thin dime fits in the fold of your pants pocket; then the other kind that hides in your bones waiting to jump out. That's the big kind of secret, the dangerous kind that requires a lock on your face. That's my kind.

My secret didn't start off that way. It started off as a small bubble of surprising joy right in the center of my chest. I first felt it the day I met Lissa flying her kite. I felt it when we were walking home together, when we sat next to each other on the school bus, or when we were at her house. It got so I couldn't wait to see her so I could feel that little bubble of joy. Pretty soon just thinking of her made it rise inside me. Was I in love with her even then? If I was, I didn't know it. And I certainly didn't think about hiding the fact that I was indescribably happy to have her as a best friend. We gave each other big bear hugs back then.

But in fifth grade, my bubble of joy had turned into a small geyser. Lissa had a habit of grabbing my hand and sticking it into her own coat pocket on the playground. That's because one of my gloves was always missing; she was trying to help keep my hands warm. When we were ten, that little gesture made me feel cozy; when I was eleven and a half, it made me feel electric. So one freezing day when she grabbed my gloveless hand on the playground and stuck it into one of her own coat pockets, I jerked away.

"What's wrong?" she asked.

"Nothing."

It felt too good, that's what was wrong. But I couldn't say that. Not that I'd ever dream of breaking off our friendship at that point. She was like my other half. But our friendship was definitely changing, at least for me. Along with the pleasure of her company, there was a slight hint of panic. Could it be that I was one of them? One of the people that Rupert called "fairies"?

Pretty insulting term, huh? Sorry. It's the only one I knew at the time. Rupert said it when we went to the ice cream parlor. Once not long after Nadine died, he and Ruby and I went to get malteds. Two men came in after we'd ordered. They sat across from each other in a booth on the other side of the room. Our malteds arrived and then their order came, too, one big double sundae with everything on it and two spoons. They began to eat out of the same dish and one of them smiled at me. I'd been staring at their ice cream. But Rupert had been staring at them. Suddenly he pulled me up out of my seat. Ruby jumped up, too.

"Come on, Orphea. We're going."

"But I haven't—"

"We're going."

He practically dragged me out of the place with Ruby scurrying behind, leaving three barely touched malteds on our table.

"I haven't finished!"

"Hush," said Ruby, "we have ice cream at home."

By now we were outside. Rupert took a deep breath. "I'm not sitting across from a couple of fairies."

I turned and looked through the window. All I could see were the two men. Their sundae was almost finished. One of them was saying something and the other was laughing. "What fairies?"

Rupert glared. "Them. Stay away from those kind of people."

The man who had been laughing noticed us staring and quickly turned away.

I got the message. There was a new kind of fairy— they were bad and also scary. I could feel the fear in

Ruby's body as she led me to the car. And the disgust on Rupert's face—as if he'd swallowed a rat. I never forgot it. So, when my hormones began to rage and my best friend became the object, you bet I felt panic.

I'm a fairy, a little voice whispered inside. What am I going to do? Then again, I thought, maybe I'm not a fairy. Maybe this is the way a person is supposed to feel when they're with their best friend in the world.

By the time we were twelve, things came to a head. Every girl in class liked a guy. Every girl except me. Even Lissa had a crush on our friend Mike. I went along with it, listening to her rave about him as if he were a rock star and she were his groupie. Not that Mike wasn't a great guy, but I didn't think he was cute. But Lissa . . .

"He has such a cute mouth! He has cute muscles! He wears his jeans in such a cute way! Don't you think?"

"If you say so."

"I think Mike would make a good father. I think we should have three children, named Amy, Keith, and Marvin."

"Yuck."

"Don't you like those names?"

"No."

"Well, help me think of some others. After all, you'll be the godmother."

I snorted. "Thanks a lot."

"What's the matter with you?" she asked. "You act as if you're jealous."

"Jealous? Me? Of course not." I couldn't admit to

that. If I was jealous of Lissa and Mike, it meant I really was a fairy.

"I think it's great that you like Mike," I volunteered. "He's cute."

Now, you may wonder where Mike came into all of this. That's the odd part. Mike didn't like Lissa at all. It turns out that Mike had a crush on me! Lissa was the one to break the news.

"I have something for you." She handed me a piece of paper folded into a tiny square.

"You wrote me a note?"

"Not me." She was pouting. Her gray eyes were angry.

"What's wrong?"

"Mike likes you! That's what's wrong. He was supposed to like me. Look at this!" She snatched the note back and read it for me. "Dear Orphea. I want to touch your velvet body!"

I laughed. "That's so corny."

"Do you like him? Yes or no?"

I thought for a minute. "Yes." I didn't like Mike in that way, of course, but I thought that I might try to. If I could like Mike, I wouldn't like Lissa, and that would be the end of my problem.

"You like him?"

"Yeah. I'm sorry."

She grabbed my hand. "That's okay. If I can't marry Mike, at least my best friend can."

"I never said I was going to marry him. And I'm not naming my kid Marvin."

"Fine," she said. "But let's just write him a note."

So the two of us carried on this love letter thing with Mike for a few weeks. It was fun. Lissa and I would write him letters together and I'd sign my name. Then he'd write letters back to me and Lissa would open them up and read them to me. Things were perfect; I was writing love letters to a boy, proof positive that I wasn't a fairy. And the best part was that since Lissa and I were writing to Mike together, I was spending even more time with her. Things came to an abrupt end when Mike wanted to go to first base.

Lissa was sick one day. Mike got off at my bus stop. He walked me up onto the porch and wham! Tongue and everything. I did my best. But he tasted like cardboard, and his lips were a little hairy.

"Sorry. I don't love you. I think we better break up."

"Okay. See you tomorrow." He wasn't too heartbroken.

After that, things fell back into place. Lissa and me; me and Lissa. She started wearing white-framed glasses then, which other people thought looked dorky. But I thought they looked great. I fell in love with those dorky glasses. I fell in love with Lissa.

Then came the rumor. It began on the school bus with two girls who sat across the aisle. They had never seemed to notice Lissa and me. It was spring of seventh grade and Lissa and I became interesting. That's what I thought. That's what you want to think when people are constantly glancing your way and whispering. You want to think that they're saying, Wow, how cool those two girls are; don't we wish we were like them? Anyway, it didn't take long to figure out that's not what they were saying. The glances became a tad sharper and the laughter a bit more sarcastic. Lissa didn't seem to notice. And I pretended not to. I hardly knew the girls' names; they weren't in class with me. What did I care what they thought? It worked, until one of them found me alone at my locker and grabbed my arm.

"Tell me one thing," she whispered in my ear. "Are you a dyke or what?"

"I don't know what you're talking about." I stared her down. I acted so cold. But inside I was shook up.

It's true, I thought. That's what I am. Only now there's a new word for it.

There was only one thing to do—be very, very careful. That way no one would ever find out.

Maybe I should have stopped being Lissa's friend then. But I didn't. Not being with her would have been like cutting off an arm. So, I was careful. I never touched her. I didn't smile at her in public. When we played softball, I didn't choose her for my team. Poor Lissa, at first she didn't understand. We'd been holding hands on the playground since the age of ten. Now I was treating her like she was poison ivy. But she came to understand without my ever explaining. Probably because when we were alone, not too much changed. When we were alone, I still gave her bear hugs; we still talked every night on the phone. When we waited alone outside the diner, she laid her head on my shoulder. And when we were together, the charge was always there.

We have a secret, I thought. A delicious and frightening secret that we share. That's what I thought. But I never asked her how she felt. I was afraid to know the truth either way. One way could mean the end of our friendship. The other way could mean something even worse: that we'd be cut off from everyone we knew—like the edge cut off a pie crust, the dough rolled into a little ball and tossed into the garbage.

■　■　■

Are you still listening? Sorry to be going on and on. How old are you out there? Some of you look about Ray's age—fourteen. Some of you look older than me. When I was fourteen, I was terrified of time. I didn't want to grow up. By then I knew I'd never be a woman in an ad for brandy. You know the kind of thing—she's in a strapless gown standing next to some tall guy with a glass of brandy in his hand, only he's not looking at the brandy, he's peeking at her boobs. Not only would I *not* be that woman worshipped and adored by a man, but when I grew up, I was going to be somebody's idea of an insult. I don't know about in your school, but in mine, one of the worst things you can call someone is "faggot" or "dyke." Not that there were any actual faggots or dykes in my school; nobody would ever own up to that, being gay I mean. I didn't own up to it either. You don't own up until you say it out loud. And I hadn't, not until that very last night. I had kept my secret locked inside. I was sixteen and my secret had grown up with me. The bubble of joy in my chest had been like a sprite, but now my secret was a giant, rattling to be let out.

That day we were at a meeting of the literary magazine. I was an assistant editor. Lissa was in charge of the art. I'd written a poem about a guy who played *djembe* in the diner. I was fascinated by this drummer's hands, how they rose and fell so swiftly, making everything pulse. She drew a picture to go with the poem— the drummer's hands.

"Perfect," I told her.

"Thanks. Want coffee?"

"Sure, let's go to the diner. Or we could go to my house. We can make coffee there." I hadn't planned on saying that.

"Are your brother and his wife at home?"

"No. They're taking tango class."

She laughed. "I can't believe it. They're so uptight."

My palms were sweating. I wiped them on my jeans. She looked away. Could she tell how I was feeling?

"If you don't want to go . . ."

She turned and smiled. "No, I want to. It's been a long time since we've been at your house."

We left school together. She had her family's old van. "Supposed to snow tomorrow."

"Maybe there'll be a snow day."

"If that's the case, I could sleep over," she volunteered.

She said it casually. Her eyes were glistening. I'd bowed out of sleepovers recently. I felt a catch in my throat.

"Sure we're not too old?"

"Never too old for a sleepover. Remember how we used to make hot chocolate?"

"Yeah."

"We can stay up all night long studying history."

"Ugh. Let's hope it does snow. Then there won't be school."

"Which means no history test."

"Then what will we do?"

I glanced out of the window. "I don't know. Chill."

I would tell her how I felt that night! I promised myself. I'd been keeping it for so long. . . .

Why am I telling you this? Because that night was so important. I've gone over it again and again. Things started to unravel as soon as we got out of the car. I was on fire, and Ruby and Rupert weren't home. We went into the kitchen and put down our books. She gave me a long look, and I kissed her.

She pushed me away.

I had read her vibes—she wanted me to kiss her, her eyes told me, her arms were beckoning. She loved me, too. But—

"What the hell do you think you're doing? Do you think I'm some kind of queer? Is this why you wanted to get me over here? So that you could embarrass me?

So that you could try and stick your tongue down my throat?"

"Sorry, Lissa. I misunderstood."

"Misunderstood what?"

"You said that after we graduated we'd go away. We'd go on a road trip."

"So?"

"You said we'd never come back, maybe, except to see your parents."

"Yeah?"

"Well, I took that for something else."

"What?"

"Love, I suppose."

She laughed. "I'm a girl. You're my friend. That's it, understand? I'm not queer."

"Okay."

"I'm not, do you hear me?"

"Okay! Okay, I heard you. So now what?"

"Now let's study."

"After this you want to study history?"

"It'll take our minds off . . . things."

"Don't you want to go home?"

"No."

So we sat in the kitchen reviewing for our history test, pretending that nothing had happened. I felt like a piece of crap.

"I'm sorry, Lissa."

She touched my hand. "It's okay. We're best friends. Nothing can change that."

"Thanks."

"Orphea?"

"Yeah?"

"I'm sorry, too."

"Sure."

"You just startled me."

"Fine."

She blushed. "Anyway, I've always wanted to try that."

"What?"

"Kissing . . . you."

I buried my nose in the history book. My heart was racing. I was so confused.

"Well, we tried it," I said, trying to make light of things. "So, that's that."

Hunched over our separate books, we kept studying. Then finally Lissa suggested that we quiz each other. Outside the snow was falling.

"You'd better get started home. The roads might get slippery."

"I'm not worried."

"Come on, Lissa, you don't want to have to dig yourself out. They probably won't send the plows out until morning."

"I don't care. I'm staying."

I gulped. "You're spending the night?"

"Sure, if it's all right with Rupert and Ruby."

"They love it when you're here. Then they don't have to deal with me."

She smiled uneasily. "I really want to stay. I'll just call home."

She called her dad. We made popcorn and hot chocolate. We opened a bag of marshmallows. Then we went upstairs and stretched across my bed, doing our favorite thing, planning our road trip. Then I heard Rupert and Ruby roll in.

"Lissa's staying over!" I called down the stairs.

"Okay," Ruby called up. "Supposed to snow all night!"

Rupert climbed the stairs. "Done your homework?" That was always the first thing he asked.

"Most of it. There may be a snow day."

"Finish it up." He tossed a smile in Lissa's direction. "Hey."

"Hey, Dr. Jones."

"Tell your dad I'm bringing in my car."

"Sure."

He turned to go. "Shovel the walk, if school is canceled. I may sleep in. That root canal I've got in the morning will probably chicken out. Any excuse to miss a trip to the dentist." He flashed a smile.

"Night, Rupert."

I closed the door. I rolled out my sleeping bag.

"You can take the bed," I told her.

"No way. I like sleeping on the floor."

"Since when?"

She glanced at me shyly. "Remember when we used to snuggle up together?"

I shrugged. "The bed's too small."

I ended up sacking out in my own bed and she lay next to me on the floor. For the first time since we'd been sleeping over together, there wasn't any talking.

"Good night, Lissa."

"Good night. Hey, Orphea?"

"Yeah?"

"I love you."

I buried my face in my pillow. She loved me. But not in the way that I loved her.

■　■　■

I woke up in the middle of the night. I felt her breath on the back of my neck.

"The floor is too hard," she mumbled. But then I felt her hand on my shoulder blade. I rolled over. She kissed me on the lips.

"Are you sure?"

"Yes. I'm sure."

"But you said—"

"I love you, Orphea."

■　■　■

Morning came. I opened my eyes. Snow was falling outside the window. She touched my foot with her toe.

"Sleep okay?" I tried to sound casual.

"Not really." Already the sun was bright.

"We slept a long time."

"Not me. I was awake, thinking."

"About us?"

"Of course."

"Are you sorry?"

"No. I can't help who I love."

"I'm scared, Lissa."

"Me too. That's why I yelled at you yesterday in the kitchen. But it's my life, Orphea. Nobody else's."

I reached over her chest and clicked on the radio. I turned up the volume. She stroked my hair. I looked into her eyes. Her eyes were laughing. We kissed and kissed again. My secret was out and it wasn't a giant. It was a beautiful rainbow.

■ ■ ■

I'm the one who started it, that afternoon in the kitchen. If she hadn't come to my house that day, she'd still be alive. It wasn't Rupert or Ruby's fault that she died. It was mine.

If I dream you, will you dream me?
Will you be my eye?
To view me on a gauzy plain,
Wrapped up in the sky?
Tell me true
And I'll tell you
What love is all about
Toss our secrets in a wishing well
And do away with doubt
So dream of me
I'll dream of you
Then we'll dream a dream of us
Seen by all who care to view
Love's haunted trust

AUNTS

Proud Road is good sleeping country. I slept for a week when I first got there, snuggled in a bed too small for me beneath Aunt Cleo's quilts. The room where Aunt Minnie put me was a loft overlooking the front of the house; the view across the road was a big field and a tilted mobile home. Other than getting up from time to time to grab a cold biscuit from the kitchen downstairs or take a trip to the bathroom, I was pretty much in a coma. On the day I finally woke up, for a minute I felt like I was in Heaven. Cozier than a sleeping bee— that's how I felt, breathing in the fragrance of woodsmoke, wiggling my toes beneath the fat covers, running my hand across the grate on the floor to feel the heat floating up from below. I lay there listening to the sounds that had already become familiar: the *clomp-clomp* of Aunt Minnie's boots as she paced, the creak of Aunt Cleo's wheelchair as she went off to the bathroom, the heavy thud of a new log on the fire, the clank of the woodstove when its door was shut. On top of that, outside it was snowing hard as a torn feather pillow. Perfect, except that Lissa wasn't there. She would have loved all that coziness, I thought. She would have gotten a kick out of the Aunts; the way Aunt Minnie chewed tobacco and spit out the juice in an old coffee can—I'd seen that the very first morning—and Aunt Cleo counting the money in the register over and over, making sure the books were balanced, I guess. Of course, there weren't any customers. A good thing, since there didn't seem to be much to sell. It was almost as if time had stopped for the Aunts; so I let time stop for me. One thing I couldn't stop, though, was the pain. Lissa was gone.

"Welcome back," Aunt Cleo said when I appeared downstairs.

I smoothed my overalls. They were even more rumpled than usual.

"Sorry I slept for so long."

"You needed it. Bed fit all right?"

"If I curl up my legs."

Her eyes twinkled. "Same bed you slept in when you were little."

"I don't remember."

"Don't you, now?"

"No. Sorry."

"Nothing to be sorry about." She wheeled across the room to the table. "Minnie is getting your breakfast. We heard you stirring."

I sat down and she placed herself across from me.

"Arthritis," she said. I'd been staring at the wheelchair.

"Sorry."

She smiled. "Wasn't your fault."

I let out a nervous laugh. "I know that. I just meant that it's too bad."

"Oh, I get by. Lucky I'm a storekeeper. My sister, Minnie, thinks the store is too confining. But it works out fine for me."

I glanced at the half-empty shelves. "Where are the groceries?"

"They'll come in the spring. In winter we don't get too many customers. And what with the canning Minnie does in summer, there's plenty for the two of us to eat."

"Hope my visit is . . . okay . . . with you," I half-stammered.

She patted my hand. "More than okay. You're family."

Then we just sat there. Have you ever just sat with somebody without saying a word? Lissa is the only one I could ever be quiet with, and that was never for more than five minutes. That kind of quiet can be unnerving. I was glad when Aunt Minnie clomped into the room. She was more the noisy type with her clomping and spitting. She grunted an awful lot, too. In fact, a grunt accompanied almost everything she did. She walked into the room and stood by the table. She put down my plate with a grunt.

"So, Lazarus has finally made an entrance."

"Lazarus?" I was confused.

"Fella who got raised from the dead," she explained. "A story from the Bible." She grunted again.

"Oh."

My stomach growled. I tried not to wolf down my eggs.

The Aunts sat across from me staring.

Aunt Cleo smiled.

"Looks just like her, for the world," Aunt Minnie growled.

" 'Deed and trust, she does," Aunt Cleo cooed.

I cleared my throat. "Who?"

"Nadine, of course," Aunt Minnie said. She put a log on the fire.

"You've got her face," Aunt Cleo told me. "You've got her smile."

I put down my fork. "I don't look anything like her. Nadine wore lipstick."

Aunt Minnie chuckled. "Yes, she did like to make herself fancy."

"I'm not like that," I protested. "I mean . . . my mother was beautiful."

Aunt Cleo nodded. "Yes, she was."

I gulped down my coffee. Why had they brought

up Nadine right away? I was already too sad about Lissa.

"Your mama's old room is next to the back door," said Aunt Minnie. She stood up and pulled out her tobacco. "You sleep there if you want to. We just put you upstairs so you wouldn't be bothered by all our noise."

"Thanks. I'm okay where I am."

Aunt Minnie crossed to the soda fountain and spit in her old coffee can. The quiet in the room turned tense.

"Those quilts you gave me are good and warm," I said, trying to make conversation.

Aunt Cleo nodded. "Made them myself. But this here's my favorite," she said, fingering the quilt across her lap. "It's a story quilt."

"It reminds me of a map."

"Every square has a story of somebody in the family."

"My mother, too?"

She nodded. "That's your mama's hand right there," she said, pointing out a square. "Traced her hand in school when she first came to live with us."

I touched the spot with my finger. It felt odd to see the shape of my mother's hand when she was a child. My own hand was so much bigger. I turned away.

"Do you remember the time you visited?" Aunt Cleo asked.

"Once . . . I remember it was snowing."

"We made snow ice cream with maple syrup," she told me. "Your mama and daddy took you and Rupert in a horse-drawn sled."

"Rupert and Daddy were here?"

"Why, sure. That bad boy Rupert tried to kill my kitty cat."

My head felt heavy. "I don't remember."

"You don't have to," Aunt Minnie said briskly. "Those times are long gone. Ain't that right, Cleo? It's Orphea that we're interested in."

I fidgeted in my chair.

Aunt Minnie peered into my face. "Rupert told us you had a problem."

"I flunked out of math."

"Is that all?" said Aunt Cleo. "That's not so bad. Boy across the road has a reading problem."

Aunt Minnie grunted. "Ain't a reason to drop out of school."

"I needed a break," I said quickly. "There were some other things, but . . ."

"Don't feel you have to tell," said Aunt Minnie. "You don't need a reason to stay with Cleo and me. You're Nadine's girl."

A lump in my throat made me scoot up from the table. Why did they keep bringing her up?

"Can I help with the dishes?"

"You can do more than help," said Aunt Minnie. "That'll be one of your chores from now on."

"And you can thread my needles for me," Aunt Cleo said cheerfully.

Aunt Minnie grunted. "And keep the fire going and split some logs."

"Split logs?" I squeaked.

"I'll teach you." She followed me into the kitchen. "Know how to make a bed?"

"Everybody knows how to make a bed."

"Everybody *thinks* they know how to make a bed. Few folks really do."

"Maybe you'd better teach me that, too."

So that's how life began for me on Proud Road. That very day I had a log-splitting lesson. I could hardly swing the ax. But Aunt Minnie did a clean cut every time, hitting the wood right on its sweet spot. I tried to guess how old she was—she was Nadine's aunt, which meant she was my great, which probably meant . . . she was in her seventies. A lady in her seventies like that, splitting wood! I was inspired. I couldn't manage to split one, but Aunt Minnie made me keep trying. My muscles were tired at the end of the afternoon, but my mind felt a little bit better. That is, until Aunt Cleo brought up Nadine again. I came through the back door, carrying the wood Aunt Minnie had split. I placed it next to the stove. Then I washed my face at the sink behind the counter. Even though it was freezing outside, I'd been sweating. Aunt Cleo watched me from her place at the register.

"You know she's right out there," she said quietly.

"Who?"

"Your mama, of course. The graveyard is in the trees right next to where you were splitting wood.

Can't see the stones, because the snow is covering them."

"Nadine is buried back there?"

"You were still a tyke, so I reckon you forgot."

"Oh, I remember being in a little church. But besides that it's only the coffin and the flowers I remember."

"I was the one who picked you up that day," said Aunt Cleo. "I picked you up when you threw yourself on the roses."

A lump rose in my throat. A lump I could hardly swallow.

"Come here," said my aunt. I crossed the room. She took my hand.

"I didn't mean to make you sad. I only thought you'd want to know that if you need her, your mama's here."

I darted away to the kitchen, biting my lip. I wasn't going to cry! I stopped in the narrow hallway under the stairs. Nadine's room was open. There were childhood pictures of her on the wall. I wanted to go in, but I couldn't.

Your face in a cloud
I on my back
You float by on the breeze
I try to shape my mouth in song
And choke on goblins' wings
Is there hearing among the dead?
Are there tears?
Do you imagine me down here?
As I translate air to hair
And force myself to see you in a cloud?
You died too soon
Bled innocence
A leaf too green
Spring into winter, no summer, no autumn
The canvas is a guillotine

GRIMES

First I met Lola. Then I met Ray. Lola is Ray's mom and my aunts' only winter customer. It's easy for her to come to Proud Store, because she lives across the road. The Grimeses and the Prouds have been neighbors forever. Only Lola isn't actually a Grimes, she just married one, a man named Jerome who got it into his head that he could have a career as a stand-up comic. Tough profession, I hear. Anyway, Ray doesn't talk about Jerome. But until he met me, Lola was his whole world. Or to put it more precisely, Ray was Lola's whole world. She let him do whatever he wanted.

A few days before Lola came swinging into the

store and introduced herself to me, I saw this boy running around across the road. I was making my bed up in the loft, trying to keep from bumping my head on the attic ceiling.

"Shit!"

"What's that?" Aunt Cleo called up.

"Sugar! I did it again!"

"Are you sure you don't want the spare room down here?"

"Nope, I'm fine."

I tucked in the quilt and looked out the window. The fields and mountains were covered with a sugar frosting of fresh snow. That's when I saw him. An apparition in a short brown coat, his hair the color of thatch, his black boots striding. I'd seen the mobile home across the way, but I assumed nobody lived there. This boy had come out of nowhere. In fact, he looked as if he'd walked out of the ground. I leaned across the bed and pressed my nose to the glass. At that instant, he looked up, first squinting into the sun, and then slightly lowering his gaze to rest on me. I ducked my head, and then bobbed back up to peek. As if he hadn't seen me (and I was sure he had!), he took off in a run down the field.

I scrunched up on my knees to get a better view. Where was he going? Was he running down to the valley? No . . . he was circling back. Running in circles, that's what he was doing! Actually, he wasn't running—he was galloping, making crazy patterns in the snow. He was slapping his side, arching his back, and tossing his head. It was quite a show. A horse show! The boy across the road was playing at being a horse! Weird . . . he looked a little old for that. I sat there watching for a long time. He seemed to never get tired. Every time he passed my way, he glanced up. An odd way of saying hello, don't you think? Obviously in need of attention, this long-legged, brown-coated boy with the shock of pale hair in his face. When he turned his back and finally galloped away, I felt exhausted.

"What are you doing up there, Orphea?" That was Aunt Minnie's voice.

"Oh, nothing."

"These shelves down here need dusting."

I hurried downstairs. The few grocery items in stock were neatly piled on the floor.

"Three tunas, two potted meats," Aunt Minnie called out.

Aunt Cleo wrote it down.

"Get a wet soapy rag," Aunt Minnie instructed.

"What are you doing?" I asked.

"Inventory," said Aunt Cleo. "We have to know what to order."

How about everything? I thought. Suppose a customer did come in? Unless they liked tuna and potted meat and needed a couple of rolls of toilet paper or had a thing for stale cupcakes, there'd be nothing to buy; except maybe some soda "pop" as my aunts called it— there seemed to be oodles of that.

"Two boxes of macaroni," Aunt Minnie announced

with a grunt. I hadn't noticed that, I guess. "The elbow kind."

Aunt Cleo sighed. "We're almost completely out of paper supplies. When you set the table, Orphea, be sparing with the napkins."

"Don't fret, Sister," said Aunt Minnie. "Your boyfriend will be here soon enough."

My mouth dropped open. "Boyfriend?"

Aunt Cleo giggled. "Minnie's just foolin'. We've got a cute delivery guy. Wears his hair in those little pig-tails."

"You mean dreads?"

"Pigtails," Aunt Minnie grouched. She didn't like being corrected. "Gray pigtails all over his head. Good-looking guy, the straw man."

"That's what we call him," Aunt Cleo explained. "Straw man, because he delivers the straws."

I wrung out my rag. "All finished. Should I put the stuff back on?"

"That's my job," said Aunt Minnie, arranging the macaroni boxes.

"Don't you think you should order before spring comes? Just in case a customer drops by?"

"We know what we're doing, Miss Orphea, thank you so much."

Right on cue, the bell on the door tinkled. I gave her a look. "Well, here's a customer."

Aunt Cleo smiled. "Shucks, that's just our Lola."

"Lola?"

"From across the road."

Lola Grimes has the reddest hair I've ever seen come out of a bottle. She's also a smoker. An unlit cigarette was clenched between her teeth and her hair was in rollers. She practically walked through me, heading for the soda fountain.

"Hey there, Miss Cleo, hey there, Miss Minnie— y'all got a match over here, I'm certain. Ray's gone and took all my matches again. I told him a trillion times to use a flashlight, even got him one of them battery-run lanterns. But the boy is stubborn. First and last, he's going to set the whole mountain on fire. Likes to paint by candlelight. But that's my boy."

The way my aunts sprang into action, you would have thought the queen of England had asked for a match.

"Well, yes indeed, Lola." Aunt Cleo put on her sweetest voice. "I'll fetch you a whole box, if you like." Her head nearly disappeared as she scooted behind the fountain.

"Can I get you some tea?" Aunt Minnie asked the redhead. "Got some water on the stove."

"I'm off tea," she announced. "Makes me jumpy. But I'll take me some coffee."

"Got a pot of that right here," Aunt Cleo sang out.

"Go bring Mrs. Grimes a cup of coffee, Orphea," Aunt Minnie prodded. "Your aunt Cleo is right by the pot. She'll pour it for you."

I did as I was told, also setting some sugar, cream, and a spoon in front of her.

"I thank ye, thank ye," Lola said with a nod.

Thank ye, thank ye? What country was she from?

Aunt Cleo took a deep breath.

"Well, now for the introductions—Mrs. Lola Grimes from across the road, meet our great-niece Orphea Proud come from Pennsylvania. Taking time out from school."

"Hello, Ms. Grimes."

"Call me Lola." She gave me the once-over. "What happened to your hair?"

"I got a short haircut. It's still growing out."

She poured some sugar into her coffee. "Never get a boyfriend with a buzz cut."

I looked at the floor. Already I didn't like her.

"So, what happened? Did you drop out?"

"Excuse me?"

"Did you drop out of school?"

"Not forever. I had trouble with math."

"I hear you. Got a boy across the road who can't read a lick." She picked up her coffee. She slurped! Maybe she wasn't that bad.

"The reason Raynor can't read is because you keep him at home," said Aunt Cleo. She pursed her lips. I'd never seen her look testy.

"My business," said Lola.

Aunt Minnie lifted an eyebrow. "Good neighbors make good fences, Cleo."

"I think it's the other way around," I added quietly. All three of them gave me a look.

"I saw a boy outside this morning. Was that your son?" I asked Lola.

"Only boy around here."

"I saw him exercising."

Aunt Minnie spit some tobacco juice into her coffee can. "Acting like a horse, you mean."

"Kind of . . ."

Aunt Cleo tugged my elbow. "Horse complex!" she said in a loud whisper. Lola pretended not to hear.

"Hear me?" Aunt Cleo whispered again. "Horse complex!"

Lola slammed down her cup. "I thought we'd been over all that."

"We have," Aunt Cleo said quickly. "Ray is your son and you know what's best for him."

"He's a talented boy," said Lola. "He ain't in school, but he keeps busy."

"In a root cellar," Aunt Minnie added.

"What does your son do?" I asked curiously. "Besides galloping?"

"He's a painter."

"House painter," chimed in Aunt Minnie. "When the weather cooperates."

"He paints more than houses," said Lola. "You just have no idea, but someday you will. The whole world will know the name of Raynor Grimes."

She put a quarter on the table and picked up the matches.

Aunt Cleo shoved the quarter back. "You don't have to pay, Lola, you know that . . . for a teeny little cup of coffee."

Lola stood up. "It's for the matches. See y'all later."

"Still working the night shift?" Aunt Minnie called after her.

"Long as I can get my car back up the hill," she answered. The bell tinkled and the door slammed.

"She's a barrel of laughs."

"Grimes," said Aunt Minnie.

"Yes, I heard. Does she work in town?"

"Chair factory. Glues legs on."

"Lola loves it," Aunt Cleo added.

"So, her son, Ray, really doesn't go to school?"

"Not since he was kicked in the head." Aunt Cleo sighed.

"Kicked in the head?"

"Yep."

"And he's really a painter?"

Aunt Minnie shrugged. "He was supposed to have done our house last summer, but it rained too much and then he got stung by a bee and Lola wanted him to paint that barn she has over there, and one thing led to—"

"I'm talking about painting. Real painting."

"Painting a house is real."

"Painting on a canvas or a piece of paper. Does Ray paint like that?"

"Lola claims he does," said Aunt Cleo.

"The only thing I know about Raynor Grimes is that he likes root beer and cupcakes," said Aunt Minnie. "Orders them every time he comes over here. Doesn't come over much anymore, though. But he loved to run across the road when he was a tyke. 'Tan I have a toot-beer and a tup-take, please?' "

Aunt Cleo laughed. "Had himself a little lisp. That Raynor Grimes was the cutest. So skinny; don't know where he put all those cupcakes, though."

I eyed the cupcakes on the shelf. "Those look a little stale."

"He's a good boy," said Aunt Minnie. "No matter how funny he acts."

"He's also your cousin," Aunt Cleo announced.

"You're kidding."

"Nope. We got Grimes blood. It's right on my story quilt." She pointed to a square with three black bars.

"No need to get into all that now, Cleo," Aunt Minnie growled.

"Why not?" I asked.

"There are some things I just don't like to talk about. That's why."

I sure understood that. "But what about this cousin deal? That boy I saw galloping looks white to me."

"Grimeses are white," said Aunt Minnie. "But the Prouds have got Grimes blood. Since all the Grimeses in Handsome Crossing are kin, that means that Ray is your cousin. That's one reason we take such an interest in him. Never know who might be in your family. Ain't it the truth?"

I thought of Rupert. Ain't it, though.

Sugar pie, oh me, oh my
Racing in the snow
Can you carve a cave in ice
Where you and I could go?
Where I might free the sweet girl's voice imprisoned in
my ear
Where kitty cats with magic paws could make grief
disappear
You and I could say our prayers and I'd get back my
knees
For another day of play, for another day of ease
Tell me how the snow dares fall
Tell me how the heat does rise
Tell me how to laugh again with a frozen spine

"P" IS FOR—

Poetry

I hadn't written since Lissa died. Not that I hadn't thought about it. I'd brought my journal with me. I still owed twenty poems to Icky and Marilyn. Luckily, I hadn't spent the two hundred dollars. But the part of me that wrote poetry had turned into a desert.

"P" is also for painting.

Lissa was a painter, and so was my new cousin Raynor Grimes.

But Ray was also a boy with a horse complex. That's what Aunt Cleo had said, and that's sure the way he acted. Every morning I saw him from my window, galloping. What a ham! He circled and pranced, even had the nerve to jump a fence. Then he looked up at me for a minute and darted away, as if he was daring me to come after him. So, I did. The problem was once I crossed the road, I couldn't find him. I knocked at the door of the mobile home. Lola answered, half asleep. She slept most of the morning, since she worked the night shift.

"Yeah?" She was wearing rollers.

"Is your son around?"

"Do you see him anywhere?"

"No. That's why I'm asking."

She stretched her arm across the door, barring my way.

"He isn't in here, if that's what you're wondering. He's in the root cellar."

"Where's that?"

She yawned and shut the door.

I circled the house looking for stairs. A cellar was like a basement. Maybe there was an outside entrance. But I couldn't find one.

"What's a root cellar?" I asked Aunt Minnie once I was back in the store.

She had opened a new pack of chewing tobacco and was storing it in a pouch. "A root cellar is just what it sounds like."

"How does it look?"

"Like a root cellar."

Aunt Cleo looked up from her sewing. "Come thread me a needle with red thread, Orphea."

I fished around in her sewing basket and quickly did what she asked.

"You have got the sharpest eye," she praised me.

"Then how come I can't find Ray Grimes?"

"Ray? Oh, he's in the root cellar."

"But *where*?"

"You sound frustrated."

"I am. I see him running in the field, then he just vanishes."

Aunt Cleo chuckled. "It's over there behind the house somewhere or another. Probably grown over with trees. It'll be close to the ground. You'll find it."

"Take him a root beer," Aunt Minnie said. "He'll guzzle that up."

I rolled my eyes. Root beer would be the perfect gift for someone who spent all his time in a root cellar. I took the can of soda from the refrigerator case, put on my coat, and crossed back over to the mobile home.

It had been freezing cold since I'd come to Proud Road. My breath froze on my face. Now I was holding an ice-cold soda, to boot. I tromped in the snow to the back of the Grimeses' house. Ray's tracks from the morning were everywhere.

I walked behind some trees and spotted a light. It seemed to be coming out of the ground! I followed it to a small window hidden behind a fallen bough. A sort of camouflage affair. The window was part of a small stone building half buried in the earth. No wonder I hadn't been able to find him. I climbed behind the fallen bough and tried the door. It was locked. But a light was on. So I knew he was in there. I remembered that Lola said he liked candles. Maybe he'd fallen asleep and was about to burn himself up.

"Ray! Are you in there?" I pounded on the door loudly. "Raaay . . . are you in they-air?" It was embarrassing. I circled round and peeked in the window. He was on the other side of the glass staring at me.

I jumped, almost dropping the root beer. "Brought you something."

He grinned and disappeared. A second later the door opened up.

I climbed down three small stone steps. Ray grabbed the soda. At first I couldn't make out what I was seeing, the light inside was so dim. He had a candle perched on a stone in the corner. I squinted, trying to get my eyes adjusted. Then I saw! He was naked except for his underwear! His pale skin was painted all over. He was a walking tattoo.

"What the hell?"

Then I noticed that the walls were painted, too. Not painted a solid color, but painted with pictures. All horses! Phosphorescent horses in yellow, purple, maroon, blue—horses floating and flying and climbing and frothing at the mouth.

"A regular psychedelic rodeo you got here!"

Ray grinned and downed his root beer. "You guessed it."

"It really is a rodeo?"

He nodded.

"It's great. You've got every wall covered. I've never seen a mural this good in my life."

"That's what Mama says."

That's when I noticed his brushes and pots of paints, scattered every which way.

"Are you some kind of mad genius?"

He looked baffled. "I took off my jeans because it gets hot in here."

"I didn't ask about your jeans. I asked if you were a genius."

"Hell no," said Ray. "I just got kicked in the head."

I got down on my knees and peered at the wall. "Mind if I light another candle?"

"I'll do it," he said, scrambling to find his pants. He pulled out some matches and lit another stubby candle. He handed me the light. Then he scurried to a corner and climbed into his jeans.

"Don't let me cramp your style," I quipped.

"No problem." When he turned around his face was red, but he didn't put his shirt on.

"You must have the metabolism of a snake. If you haven't heard, it's winter."

"It's warm down here, I promise."

"Kind of like an igloo?"

"I guess." He motioned to a couple of cushions. "Wanna set down?"

I did. "So, your mother told you who I am?"

"I reckon. Knew you were a Proud by your face."

I kind of liked that. "I'm Orphea. Thought I'd drop by. Heard you were a painter."

He tilted the soda can up to his lips. "What else did you hear?"

"That we're cousins."

"Yeah. The old ladies told me that Prouds got some Grimes in them. I'm kin to them, too, I expect. Hope you don't mind."

"No . . . how about you?"

"Fine with me. Always wanted more relations. Them rich Grimeses who live down in town don't want nothing to do with me. I'm glad to have a cousin, hope 'n' die I am."

"What's that? You hope to die?"

"I said *hope 'n' die*—it's just an expression."

"Oh, I get it—as in 'cross my heart and hope to die'?"

Ray scratched his head.

"Forget it." I settled back and looked at the paintings. "I think your horses are incredible! They're so alive. And they're really weird! I don't know why horses aren't purple for real. I think it's a good idea. Lissa would like them."

He tossed his straw-colored head. "They aren't meant to be like real life. I'm not simple, if that's what you're thinking. Who's Lissa, anyway?"

"My friend."

He gave me the once-over. "So, how come you've been spying on me?"

"Me? What about you? Don't tell me you weren't doing all that galloping for my benefit."

His eyes gleamed. "Oh, galloping is just a habit. I did gallop a little fancier because you were watching."

"I knew it!"

He sat down in the middle of the floor. He dipped a paintbrush into maroon paint. I stared at his back. It was decorated all over with a small crescent design.

"Are those tattoos on your back?"

"No, paint. I did it myself with a piece of sponge. Horseshoes."

"You sponge-painted your back with horseshoe designs?"

"Glued the sponge to a back scratcher. Looked at my back in the mirror while I was painting."

"You really do have a horse complex."

"Horseshoes are good luck," he snapped. "Don't know what you mean by complex."

"You got to admit, it's odd for a person to gallop around every morning and spend the rest of his time painting his back with horseshoes."

"Odd for a person to spend all her time staring out the window, too."

"I don't spend all my time that way," I protested.

He gave me a look. "You dropped out of school. Mama thinks you're sad because you're pregnant."

"That's ridiculous!"

"Well, how come you ran away here, then?"

"My brother kicked me out," I blurted. "But don't tell my aunts—it's a secret. And don't tell your mother."

He turned back around and began painting a hoof.

"Did you hear me?"

"Yeah. It's a secret. I understand. Now I have to paint, if you don't mind."

"Sure. I'll just watch."

I curled up my legs and watched him paint. No wonder he was hot. His arms went fifty miles an hour. He painted over things he'd already done. I heard Lola's car peel out. Then around four it began to turn dark. Outside the wind was whistling. Ray stopped to light more candles.

"When do you eat supper?" I asked him.

"In a while. Mama leaves something for me on the stove in the house."

I stood up. "Thanks for letting me stay. I have to go help my aunts." I opened the small wooden door. "See you out the window."

"Want to come galloping?"

"I don't think so. But . . . can I come back here? I'll bring you another root beer."

"How about a cupcake?"

"Are you sure? Those cupcakes at our store are mighty stale."

"That's the way I like them."

"Hey, Ray . . . you're funny."

"Thank ye, thank ye."

"You're welcome. Hope 'n' die."

■ ■ ■

I went the next day and the day after that. Watching him paint was like being swallowed by magic.

Then one day I brought my journal. Since I was spending so much time there, I figured I might as well do something. But all I did was bite my pencil. Then I began scribbling a word. The same word over and over.

"What are you writing?"

"Somebody's name."

"Lissa's?"

"How did you guess?"

"I don't know, I just did. If you miss her so much, why don't you call her?"

"I can't."

"Why not?"

"I just can't, that's all." I fumbled through my journal. I'd tucked a picture of her in the back. "Want to see what she looks like?"

He reached for the photo.

"It's an old one, from ninth grade. But it still looks pretty much like her."

He studied the picture for quite a while, then gave it back. "She's pretty."

"Her eyes are gray. You might not be able to tell from that."

"My eyes are gray, too."

I peered at his face. "I hadn't noticed. So how come you're not in school?" I asked, changing the subject.

"Have trouble reading."

"That's no reason to drop out."

"You dropped out on account of your math."

"Oh . . . right . . ."

"That's a lie, huh?"

"Look, there are some things I can't talk about. Let me ask the questions."

"Okay."

"How did you get kicked in the head?"

"That's easy. A horse did it."

"So that's why you paint horses?"

"It's only one horse I paint, just all in different colors."

I looked at the mural. "There is something about the eyes that's the same."

Ray nodded. "His name is Saint. He's scared."

"How come?"

"He knows he's going to get shot."

"Mind explaining?"

His fingers dripped green. He wiped them off with a sponge. He covered his legs with a blanket.

"When I was eight years old, I went to a rodeo with Mama and Jerome. I went off by myself to the corrals, while they were winning me a stuffed animal.

"There was a real powerful horse named Saint. He was a star in the rodeo. He was snorting and pawing the ground like crazy. His leg was tethered. So, I hopped in to help him."

"You hopped into a corral at a rodeo? No wonder you got kicked in the head!"

"Folks were scared of Saint. But for some reason I wasn't. When I climbed into the corral, he calmed down. He let me on his back. I was going to ride him."

"Are you telling the truth or is this some kind of tall tale?"

"I was on his back for just a minute. I whispered in his ear. Then I got off his back and kneeled down next to his foot. He got spooked and kicked me. After that, I went to the hospital. I didn't wake up for a long time."

"Man, you could have been killed!"

"I was trying to let him go free. Saint was a good horse."

"Where is he now?"

"People got upset with Saint. They thought he'd set out to kill me. They said he was crazy and good for nothing, so they shot him. And it wasn't even his fault."

"It wasn't yours either, Ray," I told him. "You were just trying to help. You were a little kid."

"He was beautiful. That's what I whispered in his ear. 'Saint, you are beautiful.' "

"Did your brain get hurt?" I asked quietly. "Was there damage?"

"I expect, though I can't tell the difference. Anyway, Lola says I missed so much school, I'd never catch up in reading. Since I have a talent at painting, I might as well do that."

"You are very talented. At least I think so."

"Would Lissa think so?"

"Yes."

Ray touched the wall with his brush and painted a blue mane.

■ ■ ■

One evening, Lola caught me out in the yard. "You're spending a lot of time with my boy."

"I like his paintings. Anyway, he's my cousin."

"Don't go foolin' around."

"With Ray? He's a kid."

"So are you, missie."

I stood taller. "I'm sixteen."

"And little Ray is mighty cute. I saw you with him through the window. Ray was near naked."

"He gets hot," I explained. "I'm not going to tell him how to dress when he paints. Besides, I'm not remotely interested in dating my fourteen-year-old cousin. Another thing—I'm not pregnant. Ray told me that's what you think."

"Still waters run deep. Why are you here? It ain't because of your math."

"I'm here because my aunts want me here." It wasn't exactly the truth, but it's something I'd come to believe.

"Sorry to get your back up. I worry 'bout Ray. He needs protecting."

■ ■ ■

It was about two weeks later. I finished my chores for the day, scouring out the oven in the kitchen and setting the mousetraps. I grabbed the last of the root beer out of the refrigerator case. When I closed the door to the case, Aunt Cleo's head popped up. She was over by the cash register, snoozing as usual, wrapped up in her quilt. "Can I help you?"

"It wasn't a customer, Cleo," Aunt Minnie said. "Just Orphea running across the road as usual."

"When is the soda delivery coming?" I asked. "We're out of root beer."

Aunt Minnie grunted. "Spring. He'll drink ginger ale, I reckon. Next time take him one of them."

The day was overcast but not as cold. I'd been on Proud Road for six weeks. The daylight was lasting longer. Ray and I had fallen into a routine. Every day after chores, I went over. He painted. I sat. The whole idea of writing had gone down the tubes. This particular day when I got there, something unusual occurred. The door to the cellar was padlocked. Whenever Ray locked his root cellar it was always from the inside.

I knocked. "Hey, Ray! It's me! Are you in there?"

He stepped out from behind a tree. He wasn't wearing his coat. He did, however, have on his shirt and jeans.

"Good morning. Going for a gallop? Didn't see you out here earlier."

There was a glint in his eye. "I was up all night."

"Painting horses?"

"Not exactly."

He unlocked the padlock on the cellar door with an old iron key. "Didn't want to take a chance on you getting here before I woke up."

"What's going on?"

He propped open the door with a loose rock. The cellar walls were washed with light. To my right, I saw the usual horses. But directly to my left I saw something that hadn't been there before. A life-size girl with pale gray eyes, taking up a whole wall! I drew in a breath. Lissa!

"How did you do that, Ray?"

He had gotten her just right!

"You showed me her picture, remember? But then she kind of painted herself."

"She looks so alive."

"Glad you like it."

He'd managed to capture the light in her eyes, her moon-shaped face, her long arms and thick black braid . . . she was wearing an orange blouse.

"Orange was one of her favorite colors. How did you know?"

"I didn't. Color just goes good with her hair."

I felt a stab in my chest. "I miss her, Ray."

"That's what you keep saying. Ask her to come for a visit. She can stay with us, if your aunts ain't got the room. She can sleep in my bed."

"Thanks, that's sweet. But there's a reason she can't visit. She died."

He hung his head. "Why didn't you say so?"

"It's a secret. Don't tell my aunts, okay? And don't tell Lola."

"If that's what suits you."

I sat down in front of the portrait. I couldn't stop looking at her, even though it hurt.

Ray scooted for the door. "I'm going to my house. I ain't brushed my teeth."

"Want to know another secret, Ray? . . . I loved her."

"Same way I loved Saint?"

"Sort of . . ."

The tears I'd saved up since I came to Proud Road began to trickle out.

■　■　■

That night I tossed and turned in the little bed in the loft. Seeing Lissa in the root cellar looking so alive made me remember how happy she made me; and that made me remember that she was gone. I got up and tiptoed downstairs. Aunt Cleo and Aunt Minnie were sound asleep in their room, both of them snoring. The only light came from the glowing embers in the potbellied stove and the half-moon out the window.

I felt my way to Nadine's room and sat stiffly on the side of her bed. The room smelled like musty lavender. Was that the way she had smelled? I tried to remember. She had smelled like . . . herself. But what was that? I began to cry again. The memory of her fragrance had disappeared. I peered at the walls covered with pictures of Nadine as a child. Since I'd shied away from coming into her room, I hadn't yet gotten a good look at them. And now it was too dark to see. But I could feel her all around me. . . .

She had lived in this place before I existed. She'd gone away and had me. Then she'd left the world. And me.

Mom, some things can't be forgiven
The orange skirt put out in a bag
Never mind it was ruined
Your voice turned to vapor
The thousand braids, the hugs
All gone
Yet I remain to blow out my candles
Year after year, clenching in my fist
The same futile wish
That you were here

THE GIG

Not long after that, I started writing. My brain was wormy with words; I couldn't get them down fast enough. Ray was on to a new mural as well, so things were even hotter down in the root cellar. He white-washed one of the walls and the ceiling and started all over with more Saint variations—that's how I came to think of them. The portrait of Lissa he left; she was just in the middle of a rodeo was all. Sometimes Ray would ask me what I was writing. It was hard to say. I seemed to be blatting out my whole life onto the page. I wrote about Nadine and Daddy, Rupert and Ruby; mainly about losing Lissa, though. Most of the poetry was about that. After a while, I had quite a few poems. I had no idea that someday I'd share all that stuff I was writing with all of you. I began thinking a lot about Icky and Marilyn. I hadn't been in touch with them since the day they told me about leaving for Queens. So I tried their cell number. Icky picked right up.

"Hey, kiddo! Where did you disappear to? We called you before we left, but your brother said you were visiting relatives. Wouldn't give us your number."

"I'm with my aunts down in Virginia. Sorry I didn't call you myself. I was in the dumps for a while."

"No more fertility pills, I hope?"

I chuckled. "Nothing like that."

"So, written any poems?"

"I haven't forgotten that I owe you."

"Don't worry about it."

"How's it going in Queens?"

"We got a place to stay and the whole bit. Renovating an old warehouse for the club. Going to call it Club Nirvana."

"Cool. Well, I just wanted you to know that I have written a few poems, not twenty, but getting there."

"Coming up this summer?"

"I don't know."

"Got to read your poems at the open mike."

"I'm not sure they're good enough, Icky. And . . . I don't know if I feel like going anywhere."

"I hear you. Lissa's death will take time to get over, I expect."

"I could mail you the twenty poems when I'm done."

"No hurry."

"I'm writing some other stuff, too."

"Such as?"

"The story of some of the things I've been through . . . the story of Lissa and me. I'm not sure I want to read that at an open mike, though."

"Listen, kid, you do whatever you like. But if you want a gig this summer . . ."

"A gig? A real gig?"

"You heard me. If you're not up for it, you can just come and help me with the lights. Marilyn and I think you're great, kiddo."

"I think you're great, too, Icky. Here's my aunts' telephone number and address in case you want to reach me."

After that call, I wrote even faster. I wasn't sure what I was thinking. I could never talk about what happened with Lissa and me in public! I thought I'd just send them my poetry. Or someday when I wrote about something else, I might accept that gig at Club Nirvana.

Out of my way, Giant
I've got bumblebees on my side
They'll sting you with honey
And steal all your money
They'll tan your hide
Now I don't mean to threaten
But love is a weapon
It can slay you good as a gun
So out of my way, Giant
Your lazy day is done

PUZZLE

Do you ever feel like your life is a puzzle? Sometimes I do. A few months after arriving at Proud Road, I really felt like that. There were so many pieces of me floating around: me and Lissa, me and Nadine, me and Daddy; me and my aunts and me and Ray, me and poetry and Icky and Marilyn; my old life with Rupert and Ruby and my new one on Proud Road. And then there was the biggest puzzle piece of all, being "gay." I say it was the biggest piece because so much space inside me was taken up in hiding it. I was hiding, no getting around it. I'd gone as far as telling Ray about Lissa, even told him I loved her. But I was pretty sure he didn't get the actual gist of what I meant. And Aunt Cleo and Aunt Minnie—I'd kept them totally in the dark. They still thought I left home because of some problem with math. I tried to convince myself that I didn't talk with them about Lissa and my being gay because I didn't want to upset them. The truth is I was scared. I was pretty certain they wouldn't knock me upside the head the way Rupert had; but suppose they asked me to leave? Suppose they didn't like me anymore? Some people might call that a chickenshit way of thinking. Be who you are—if others don't like it, screw them. But suppose you really, really care about somebody? And what if they find out something about you to make them not want to know you anymore? Or even be afraid of you as if you're some kind of freak? I cared a lot about Aunt Cleo and Aunt Minnie. I couldn't chance losing them.

Spring came. Icicles cracked from the eaves of the store, making big puddles. Runoff from the melting snow left the road with even more ruts. Lola's car got stuck coming out of her driveway four times a week. Ray and I gave her a push every time.

"This mud is worse than the snow," she'd mutter, skidding off down the mountain.

Over at our place, my aunts began their spring cleaning. I helped them take down the lace curtains and wash them gently in the bathtub. Then Aunt Minnie and I hung them out in the sun to dry on a clothesline strung between two trees. Aunt Minnie and I took everything off the shelves while Aunt Cleo did a final inventory. There were lots of stale cupcakes left, which we crushed up to add to some chicken feed. Aunt Cleo explained that every spring they bought a few chicks.

Across the road, Ray spring-cleaned for Lola, running the vacuum and washing the windows. She'd decided she wanted a paint job on the mobile home and had settled on lavender. So, Ray had to postpone our daily meetings in the root cellar. Sometimes I went over alone; I'd gotten so used to writing there. Lissa's portrait was still on the wall, but when we weren't in the cellar, we kept her covered with a sheet. Ray was cooperative about that. Even though he was dying to show off the painting, he'd even kept it from Lola, because I'd asked him to.

Every day after he was done painting their home, Ray took to coming to the store. He'd gone through the rest of the ginger ale and was working on a case of orange pop. He was kind of mad when he found out we were planning to use the stale cupcakes to feed our chickens. Sometimes he stayed for supper. But he still saved time for galloping. Sometimes I even joined him, but I couldn't actually bring myself to gallop. Even though no one was looking, I was afraid to act like a fool. So instead of galloping next to Ray, I jogged.

There were lots of logs to split in the spring. We'd gone to the end of the woodpile and it was so chilly we still used the stove. Time and again Aunt Minnie coached me, but I still hadn't hit the sweet spot. I'd take a log from under the porch and lean it up against a stump. I'd hit it with the ax, and the ax would get stuck. Aunt Minnie would watch me, chuckling.

"What am I doing wrong?"

"You've got to develop a feel for it. Once you hit that sweet spot, your troubles will be over."

On a day when the first warm breeze was licking my face, I finally made a clean cut and split a huge log in two.

"I found it!" I cried, jumping up and down. "I found the sweet spot!"

All the snow vanished, except on the tippy-tops of the mountains. My legs got so restless! I walked up and down the road. Then I walked into the woods beyond the spot where I'd been splitting logs. The markers in our family graveyard peeked up through dark, soggy leaves along with some tiny white crocuses. My heart beat faster. This was the place where they'd lowered Nadine's coffin into the ground. I tried to remember the details, but I couldn't. Where was the mountain that I had seen? Where was the spot where they had lowered her? I got down on my hands and knees looking for her name. PROUD was on all the markers, but I didn't see Nadine's.

"She's under the tree," a voice said behind me. It was Aunt Minnie. She was standing there in a jacket and work boots.

"You and I were thinking the same thing," she said.

"Oh, I didn't mean to come here." I got up quickly.

"Well, this is your mama's." She pointed out a spot

a little apart from the rest. "She used to like to climb that tree. So we put her under it."

I crossed to the stone. My eyes scanned what was written on it. NADINE PROUD, 1970–1996. I turned away quickly.

"She played in the graveyard? That's spooky."

"There wasn't much your mama was afraid of. A few ghosts wouldn't have scared her."

"Right. She did what she wanted to. That much I remember."

"Your grandmother and grandfather are over where the rest of them are buried."

My palms began to sweat. "Nadine never talked about them much. I can't even remember how they died."

"Train accident. My brother Thomas, your grandfather, was a porter. Good job. He took your grandmother Cassie on a trip to Chicago. Thomas was going to have a layover there and he thought they might as well . . . Anyhow, they left your mama with us when they went on their trip. After they died, she just stayed on. She was only ten. It was hard on her."

The sun ducked behind the clouds. I suddenly felt cold. "Some family—I'm in a long line of dead people."

"Some of us are still hanging on."

"Nadine died so young. Does that mean I'll die young?" I joked.

"Your life is all your own. It doesn't have to be like your mother's."

A taste like iron came into my mouth. "You would

think that Nadine would have tried to hold out a little longer—she knew what it was like to lose her own parents. She could have waited at least until I was eighteen before she died, instead of leaving me with that jerk brother of mine."

"She loved you."

"You know she used to sing opera? She went to this guy's apartment and took me with her. Daddy didn't know anything about it. After Daddy died, she didn't sing opera anymore. She developed these headaches and could hardly get out of bed. She stared off into space. She couldn't read a simple bedtime story."

"Could be that she was sick for longer than we knew. If only Cleo and I had lived closer, we could have checked on her. When your father died, she was heartbroken."

"She loved him?"

"You don't remember?"

"I remember him throwing the radio in the sink."

Aunt Minnie sighed. "Most couples have squabbles. But for Nadine the sun rose and set in Reverend Apollo Jones."

"He was so much older," I protested. "He robbed the cradle."

"Oh, he loved her all right! Loved her voice. She sang in the choir at the church. Nobody could touch her when she sang 'His Eye Is on the Sparrow.' And Reverend Apollo Jones just couldn't help himself. Already married with a son . . ."

"Did people gossip?"

"Yes, indeed. It was a scandal."

"But Daddy married Nadine anyway?"

Her gaze turned hard. "Nadine went after him. We tried to get her to act right. But when she wanted something, she went after it."

My eyes smarted with tears. "Guess she wanted to be with him more than she wanted to be with me. As soon as he died, she died, too."

"Don't be bitter, Orphea. If your mama died of a broken heart, it wasn't because she wanted to leave you behind."

"Then why did she die?"

"Like I said, maybe she was sick for longer than we knew. Could have had a brain tumor growing. Or maybe she wasn't as strong as we all thought."

"You've got to be kidding. Nadine was the strongest person I've ever known. She did whatever she wanted to."

Tears welled up inside me. I fought them back. I knew I was demanding explanations for something that couldn't be answered. And I couldn't help it.

I felt Aunt Minnie's callused hand grip my shoulder. "If Nadine was strong, you're stronger."

"Then why do I feel so weak?"

■ ■ ■

You know how when things are bad, the littlest thing can pick you up?

Ray had finished the mobile home. Lola was ecstatic.

"My boy is the best painter! Ain't it pretty?"

"Gorgeous!" said Aunt Cleo. "Indeed and trust, I've never seen light purple I liked better, except maybe the color of lilacs."

"Think Ray could spruce up our place?" Aunt Minnie asked. "We can pay him soon as we get a ride down to the bank."

"I'll tell him," said Lola.

So Ray began to paint the store. Aunt Cleo wanted it pink like it always had been, but Aunt Minnie insisted on yellow.

"We need a change around here," she said firmly. "Getting tired of looking at the same stuff." The following Saturday, Lola went to the hardware store in town and picked up some yellow paint. She got a small can of shiny black as well, so that Ray could spruce the sign up.

"I wanted it painted pink like always," Aunt Cleo muttered. "Don't know why you have to always get your way, Minnie."

"Because I'm oldest," Aunt Minnie said, spitting into her tobacco juice can.

■　■　■

One day, while I was out on the porch with Ray, helping him mix paint, Aunt Cleo wheeled herself over and nabbed me.

"Lookee here," she whispered, grabbing my elbow.

"Something you'd like, Aunt Cleo?"

"Want to show you something."

I came closer.

She tugged at her story quilt. "Can't let Minnie get wind of this."

"Aunt Minnie is in the back, clearing out her garden."

Ray looked up curiously.

"You can hear, Ray," said Aunt Cleo. "This concerns you, too."

We sat at her feet. She took the story quilt off her shoulders and spread it on her lap.

"See this here patch on the quilt with the three black bars? Those bars are an iron gate."

"Yes, ma'am," said Ray.

"You pointed that square out to me once before," I told her.

She nodded. "It's for our Grimes relative. Your great-great-grandfather whose body got stolen!"

"Stolen? He's not buried out back with the rest of the family?"

She shook her head.

"Who stole his body?" asked Ray.

"Hate to say this, Ray. But it's your people."

"I didn't steal no corpse, now . . ."

"Of course not, boy. Not saying you did. But he was Grimes and when he died, the Grimeses came to take him away."

"Why?" I asked.

"Use your brain, girl—he was white and so are they."

I glanced at Ray. His face had turned red.

"It was the rich Grimeses," added Aunt Cleo.

"Oh, well, that's a different branch altogether," Ray said, perking up.

I still felt uneasy. "Why are you mentioning it, Aunt Cleo? It's in the past. Why don't we talk about some of the other squares in the story quilt?"

"Because it isn't in the past! Minnie and I promised our own father that we'd go to where the Grimeses are buried."

"Where's that?"

Her eyes got wider. "In the white cemetery."

"What kind of cemetery is that?"

"The segregated kind."

"Maybe you better start at the beginning, Aunt Cleo."

"My father's mother was Gabriella Proud. She married a man named Grimes. She was black and he was white. Of course, it wasn't legal for different races to get hitched in them days.

"But my grandmother Gabe, that's what they called her, was going to be her own person and love who she wanted and she loved this white fella. From the rich branch of the Grimes family."

Ray snorted. "This means I had nothing to do with it."

"Are you sure you have this straight?" I asked Aunt Cleo. "The stories I hear about white men and black women in the old days—"

"This isn't one of those," she said. "This is a real love story. She loved him and he loved her, too. That was my father's father, you see. And my father told me all about it. Gabe and Babe, that's what they called him, liked to read, liked to garden, both good-looking. They got married even though they weren't supposed to, with a preacher and everything."

"How?"

"Beats me, but they did it. Got the marriage certificate on record in town."

"Get to the part about the body stealing," Ray prodded.

Her eyes twinkled. "So, Gabe Proud and Jameson Grimes—Babe's first name was Jameson, Babe was just his nickname—well, they got married and had a family. But when Babe Grimes died his sister came to claim his dead body. 'You had him in life, but you will not have him in death,' she said."

"How do you know all this?" I asked.

"Handed down."

"Tell us the rest," said Ray.

Aunt Cleo smoothed out the quilt. "This Grimes sister and her husband took my grandfather Babe to be buried. They put him in the white cemetery. Daddy was a teenager at the time. They wouldn't allow Grandma Gabe to go to the funeral. But they allowed his son to go. But when he left, they shut these iron gates on him.

" 'We let you come to the funeral, Eugene Proud, but don't think you're ever coming back in here again!'

" 'But that's my daddy!' said Eugene. 'I got to visit his grave to pay my respects.'

" 'Don't step foot in here, young Proud. If you do, you and all your family will be mighty sorry!' "

"So, your father never went back?" I asked.

"He never did," Aunt Cleo said sadly. "In those days, that was serious stuff. Worst case, he could have been shot if he went back through those gates."

"That makes me mad," said Ray. "I don't want to be a Grimes, if they're that mean."

"Doesn't matter how mean they are now," I piped up. "Now nobody can keep you out of a cemetery because of your race. We have laws."

"Minnie and I can't go through those gates," Aunt Cleo said quietly.

"Why not?" said Ray. "Mama will give you a ride to town. You can go visit your grandfather's stone on a Saturday sometime."

She shook her head. "Minnie will not hear of our going. I've begged her. During my own father's lifetime, he couldn't go through those cemetery gates. He was afraid; he had been threatened. He made me and Minnie promise him that we would go visit our grandfather's grave for him. Our daddy asked us that just before he died. I promised him, Orphea, that I would do it. And Minnie promised him, too. But Minnie is still afraid. No matter what she promised, no matter how times have changed, she won't walk through those gates."

"But what can I do?"

"Go find the grave. Go to town. You and Ray can do it. The white cemetery is just over by the big grocery store. Pay respects to your ancestor for your aunt Minnie and me. Tell him he doesn't have to hover anymore."

A shiver went through my body. "He hovers?"

"We feel his presence sometimes. He's been waiting a long time for his family to come visit him. If you go to the cemetery, his spirit will be at peace and pass on."

"I'll do my best, Aunt Cleo."

"Thank you, Orphea. Whatever you do, don't tell Minnie."

■ ■ ■

"Lola, if you pass by the paper factory, tell the straw man that we've been waiting on him for nearly a month!" Aunt Minnie yelled.

"Don't forget to pick up that thread for me, Orphea," Aunt Cleo cried out. "And some peanut brittle from the candy store, bunion pads from the pharmacy, and some bakery bread and pickles! Tell them to put it on our account! See you later!"

"See you later!" I called with a wave.

It was another Saturday and Ray and I were going into town with Lola. Owning a general store didn't prevent my aunts from being out of practically everything. Ray wanted to linger in every store—it had been so long since he'd been to town. The candy store took forever. I told Ray I'd buy us a treat with my money. He couldn't decide whether he wanted chocolate with pecans or marshmallows. We ended up buying some of each. Then we hopped into the car with Lola again and headed for the five-and-ten, where Lola bought Ray some art supplies and I got myself a black-and-white composition book. I'd been writing so much that my journal was all filled up. Then we made our way toward the cemetery, the "white" one where my Grimes ancestor was buried. Though we hadn't told Aunt Minnie, we had let Lola in on our plan. She was happy to help.

"It's time the old ladies put that story to rest. It seems to weigh heavy on them. Besides, Jameson Grimes is Ray's ancestor, too. Locating the grave would be nice for us all."

Lola knew just where the "white" cemetery was. She let me and Ray off at the grocery and pointed us in the right direction. "Just around the corner from the parking lot. You'll see some shiny brass gates. Meantime, I'll drop in on the straw man."

Within five minutes of leaving her, Ray and I came upon a modern-looking graveyard. The gates were wide open. An office was right off the entrance. Through the glass door we could see a lady in a flowered dress sitting behind a computer. She smiled and motioned us in. Though she looked middle-aged, she had a perfectly smooth face. In my mind, I called her Mrs. Peach Face.

"Help you?"

"Yes, please," I said. "We're looking for the grave of a Jameson Grimes. Would have been buried here about eighty years ago."

Her little face lit up. "One of the old ones!"

"Our relative."

She looked at Ray, and then looked at me. "Related to both you and him?"

"Well, that's what my aunts say."

"This is my distant cuz," Ray boasted.

Mrs. Peach Face turned to her computer and keyed something in. "I'll look up the name."

"Ray and I just found out that we were cousins recently," I couldn't help chiming in.

"And y'all found each other? This kind of thing is happening more and more. Different branches of the same families connecting up. Rest a spell. I'll see what I can find for you."

Ray and I busted open the candy. Mrs. Peach Face lit on her computer like a flea on an elephant, finding Jameson Grimes's location before we could finish the chocolate with marshmallow.

"He's way around the back of the hill, in the old part of the graveyard. Best way to reach it is to walk around the corner. You'll see another set of gates. But it's just as easy to climb over the wall."

"Thank you."

"Good luck."

We found him! Walked around the corner and up the hill. The second set of gates was black, just like on Aunt Cleo's quilt. The gates were choked shut with weeds and wildflowers. So Ray and I hopped the stone fence and started looking. It took a little while, because for some reason Jameson Grimes was in a plot with some people called Gallitan. At least, all the other stones in the plot had the name Gallitan on them except his. It took Ray's eagle eye to find him.

"How come he's in with the Gallitans? The rest of the Grimeses are over there under the cherry tree."

"Who knows? But this is his marker. It says Jameson Grimes on it."

Unlike the fancier stones in the Gallitan plot, Great-great-grandfather Grimes's marker was stubby and plain, without a verse or fancy lettering.

"Just wait until we tell Aunt Cleo and Aunt Minnie!"

"Ain't supposed to tell Miss Minnie," Ray reminded me.

■ ■ ■

When we got home and I gave Aunt Cleo the news, she smiled so hard I thought her face would break open.

"The lady who works in the office was nice to us," I told her. "You can go to see the grave yourselves. Lola says she'll drive you!"

"Drive Cleo where?" I hadn't seen Aunt Minnie behind the soda fountain.

"I asked Orphea to find Grandpa Babe Grimes's grave," Aunt Cleo said bravely. "And she and Ray did!"

Aunt Minnie's mouth dropped open. "In the white cemetery?"

"I don't think it's a white cemetery anymore, Aunt Minnie."

"My father was told never to enter those gates."

"That was a long time ago."

"Lola will take us to town, Minnie. If the children could walk through the gates, we can, too. Please, we promised we'd pay our respects."

Aunt Minnie finally gave in.

■　■　■

The following Saturday, Lola drove us back into town, this time with my two aunts. Mrs. Peach Face was in the cemetery office. I found out her real name—Mrs. Graves! Weird, right?

"These are my aunts. They own a store on Proud Road."

Aunt Cleo and Aunt Minerva nodded shyly.

"Proud Road! Used to go up there as a girl. Had a nice apple orchard."

"That belonged to our family," Aunt Minnie said. "Afraid it's grown over these days."

"Oh, used to be a lot of timber up that way when I was a girl," Mrs. Graves went on. "A little bitty store almost on top of the mountain."

"That's us!" Aunt Cleo said, grinning with pleasure.

"Well, your niece knows where the grave is." Mrs.

Graves smiled at Ray and me. "Such a nice human-interest story—having the cousins find each other. My daughter writes stories for the newspaper."

"Do tell," said Aunt Cleo. "Well, our niece writes very good poetry." I'd never read her any of my poems, but she'd asked what I'd been writing in my journal.

"Such a coincidence," said Mrs. Graves. "And is your cousin also a writer?" she asked, nodding in Ray's direction.

"He's a painter," Aunt Minerva boasted. "A right smart one! I ain't seen any of his picture-type paintings, but I do know he paints houses well."

"He paints beautiful horses!" Lola chimed in from where she'd been standing back near the door.

"I'll have to come up that way and pay y'all a visit," said Mrs. Graves.

After all the formalities, we drove around the corner. Ray and I had to get the iron gates unstuck to wheel in Aunt Cleo. So we pulled up the weeds and wildflowers. When the gates were unchoked, we opened them wide enough to push the wheelchair inside. Then Ray, Lola, and I lifted it up to carry Aunt Cleo over the markers, because the aisles were so narrow. When we set Aunt Cleo down in front of Jameson Grimes's tombstone, Aunt Minnie was still outside the gate.

"Come on, Miss Minnie," Lola called.

She shook her head no.

"Why not?" I ran over.

She cupped her hand to my ear and whispered: "Scared . . ."

I put my hand on her shoulder. "What are you scared of?"

"Been afraid of these gates all my life. Those people told my father not to come in here. Besides, my legs are wobbly."

"Take my hand. I'll walk with you. You've come all this way. You should see the grave." She took a small step, then walked through, holding on to my arm.

Once they were there, my aunts didn't want to leave. There were prayers to say, and they wanted to catch up on old times with their grandfather, especially Aunt Cleo.

"We finally came to see you, Grandpa Babe," she cooed. "We would have been bringing flowers all these years but they wouldn't let us. But Minnie and I will be coming from now on. Say something, Minnie—"

"Say what? He's dead."

"You never know, his spirit might be listening. You could say a word or two."

"About what?"

"Anything that might be of interest."

Aunt Minnie cleared her throat. "Hello, Grandpa Babe . . . it's Minerva Proud speaking. That well you dug will have plenty of water this summer on account of all the snow this year. If you're wondering, your wife's family store is still going, though it's doing poorly. Called Proud Store like always. Your son

Eugene and his family went back to the Proud name after you died. Your Grimes relations took their name away when they took your body. Matter of factly, though, we got a young Grimes with us today. Name of Raynor. Not from your branch, but you're all kin. We also brought Orphea. Cleopatra and I thought we might be the last of the Prouds in these parts, but then young Orphea came to live with us."

Aunt Cleo reached down and touched the stone. "Rest now, Grandpa."

In the car on the way back to Proud Road, Aunt Cleo offered a theory on why Jameson Grimes's marker was in the Gallitan plot instead of being with the other Grimeses.

"His sister was married to a Gallitan," she explained. "And she's the one who came to take the body. When she fetched Grandpa Babe's body, she had it buried in her husband's plot. Probably the other Grimeses didn't want him in the big plot with all the other Grimes family members."

"Maybe they thought he wouldn't be noticed if they stuck him someplace out of the way," I suggested.

"They were ashamed of him," said Aunt Minnie. "They gave him a real plain marker compared to everyone else's."

"Why were they ashamed of him?" asked Ray.

"Because he married one of us," said Aunt Cleo.

"Plain dumbness," said Lola, "that's what it was."

■   ■   ■

After that, how could I keep my secret? I was still afraid, but hadn't Aunt Minnie been afraid? Besides, I wanted them to know me, to know me as well as I was getting to know them. By keeping my love for Lissa a secret from my aunts, I was keeping myself outside of the circle. I was keeping myself apart from what I wanted, a family.

I chose a rainy afternoon when Ray was at his own house and Aunt Minnie couldn't garden. She was sorting flower seeds at the table in front of the stove. It had warmed up enough so that we no longer needed a fire during the day. Aunt Cleo and I had just finished a round of tic-tac-toe. I put down the pencil and stood up.

"I have something to tell the two of you."

Aunt Minnie looked up from her sorting. I was facing them both.

"I'm gay. That's the reason I came here. There was no problem with math. I had a friend named Lissa. We fell in love with each other. Rupert found out and got really angry. He said we didn't have people like that in our family. I acted kind of crazy. So Rupert and Ruby drove down and dumped me here."

I waited for what seemed like an eternity.

Aunt Cleo broke the silence. "Why didn't you tell us before?"

"Rupert told me not to. He said you were righteous."

Aunt Minnie grunted. "What's that supposed to mean?"

"That you think it's a really bad thing, even a sin. Ruby told me to forget my feelings. But I can't."

Aunt Minnie got up and walked over to me. "My definition of righteous is different from Rupert's." She touched my cheek. "You're family, honey child. The fact that you're gay, as you call it, doesn't take away from that."

"Uncle Jed was gay," Aunt Cleo sang out.

"Someone else in our family?"

"At least one someone else," she said, wheeling herself over. "Bookworm Jed, we called him. He was so good to us. Never got married. Didn't talk much about being gay; people didn't talk about it then. But everybody knew. And it didn't make a bit of difference in the way we felt about our uncle."

Relief washed over me. "You don't think I'm unacceptable?"

"Of course not," said Aunt Minnie. "I worry about how other folks who don't understand these things might treat you, though. But you're strong. You know who you are."

Hearing her say that, I began to feel stronger.

"Daddy would probably roll over in his grave—that's what Rupert said."

"We'll never know," said Aunt Minnie. "I do know that your mother would have loved you even more, if that's possible."

"How do you know?"

"Nadine was a free spirit. She'd never judge a soul."

"She wasn't in the position to," Aunt Cleo added. "She lived her life just the way she wanted to."

"But she wanted to sing opera—she gave up her dreams for Daddy. That's the way it seemed to me."

"It may have looked that way to you when you were a little girl, Orphea, but I don't think that's true. Nadine's dream was to marry Reverend Apollo Jones and to have a little girl."

"Don't forget going to Kenya," Aunt Minnie reminded her. "If Nadine had wanted to leave Apollo, she wouldn't have hesitated."

"Do you really think she would have still loved me?"

"Would you let something stop you from loving her?" asked Aunt Minnie.

"No. Never."

"There's your answer."

Aunt Cleo fanned herself. "Knew there was something on your mind. Glad you finally came out with it."

"You didn't believe the story about math?"

Aunt Minnie hooted. "We weren't born yesterday, pumpkin."

"This calls for a soda pop," said Aunt Cleo, crossing to the refrigerator case.

"No ginger ale, root beer, or orange," I told her.

"Fine. I'll take black cherry. Want one?"

I sat down at the table. "Sure."

"Minnie?"

"No thanks. I'll just have me a chaw." She pulled out her tobacco pouch. "So, where's Lissa?"

"That's the other piece. She died in a car accident, just before I came down here."

"Oh, my . . . ," murmured Aunt Cleo. Aunt Minnie put her arms around me.

"You've been through a lot, girl. But we're here with you. You're home."

■　■　■

The following day the sun was out. I went over to speak with Ray and asked him to wake up his mother. I wanted my aunts to see Lissa in the daylight. Aunt Minnie and Aunt Cleo got into their best clothes for the occasion. Though Lola didn't know the whole story, she was excited about the plan.

"I'd love for them to see Ray's horses! I haven't checked in on him myself in months." She even insisted on making punch and opening a bag of cookies for the event. "This is a regular art opening," she said with a giggle.

Ray and I wheeled Aunt Cleo out onto the porch. She was wearing a pearl necklace. Aunt Minnie was carrying a big red pocketbook, which she gave to Aunt Cleo to hold while she, Ray, Lola, and I lifted the wheelchair off the porch and pushed it across the road.

"I feel just like a queen," chirped Aunt Cleo. "Leaving the store twice in the same month."

We set the wheelchair down in front of the root cellar and Ray opened the door. Aunt Minnie stepped inside and stood out of the way, so that Lola could squeeze in. There was just enough space left in the doorway for Aunt Cleo to poke in her head. Ray and I waited outside. The first voice we heard was Lola's.

"What happened to the horses?"

"I painted over them, Mama."

"Where did this girl on the wall come from?"

"That's Lissa," Aunt Cleo said quietly. "She's lovely!"

"Orphea's friend," Aunt Minnie explained.

"She showed me a photo," Ray chimed in. "Do you like her, Mama?"

"Like it a lot!" said Lola. She came outside beaming. "First time you ever painted a person. Good job!"

"She died," Ray told her.

"That's awful!"

"She wasn't only my friend, she was my girl-friend," I said.

"You're queer?"

"If you want to call it that."

She shrugged. "Oh, well. Can't help who you fall in love with. I thought I was marrying a guy with his head on his shoulders, turned out to be a space cadet. Sorry about your friend, though."

"Thanks."

When we carried Aunt Cleo back to the store, there were tears in her eyes.

"That girl could walk off the wall, she's so alive. It's like she could start speaking."

■　■　■

After supper, I went to Nadine's room and turned on the light. I looked at her baby pictures. It was hard to believe that my own mother had once been a baby. I picked up the doll on the nightstand and gave it a hug. Then I opened the drawers of her dresser. In one of them was a photo of the two of us standing in the snow with a boy. The boy was holding me in his arms. It took a minute for me to realize that it was Rupert. The photo appeared to have been taken on the same day as the one I'd always kept of me and my mother. Strange how I'd forgotten that Rupert had been with us. In the photo he looked like anybody else's big brother. What else didn't I remember? Who had taken the picture? I wondered.

In the second drawer I opened, I found a strand of pink pop beads and one of those diamond rings from a bubble gum machine. I put the jewelry on and sat down on the bed. I was waiting for some kind of sign from my mother. None came. So I got up and opened her closet. On the floor stood a small pair of white rubber boots. At that moment I heard a voice. I'm sure it came from my mind, but it was so strong and vivid; as if it came from somewhere else outside of me. But it wasn't Nadine's voice. It was Lissa's.

Hey, Duckfeet!

I smiled.

Maybe Lissa and Nadine would meet up someday, I thought. I took comfort in that.

While I slept a river grew
A winding road of roots and gloom
Wading to the other side
A splendid horse gave me a ride
From his back, I spied a cavern
The entrance cloaked with hands unfurling
Tossing off a light too bright
Your face the center, beauty blinding
I heard a whisper, turn around
My horse stepped in
I will not drown

FAME

Mrs. Graves kept her word and paid a visit. She brought her daughter with her, a much younger version of herself wearing great big rhinestone earrings and a long flowered skirt. She seemed cool, so I invited her over to Ray's museum. She couldn't stop snapping pictures. Me and Ray standing side by side; Ray, Lola, and me; Ray with the paintings he'd done of Saint on the other walls. The last one she took was of Ray and me standing on either side of Lissa's portrait.

"Tell me about the young lady in the painting," said the journalist.

"She was my best friend," I explained. "After that, she became my girlfriend," I added shyly.

That was the photo that appeared in the *Handsome Crossing Gazette*. The caption read:

> *Orphea Proud and Raynor Grimes of Proud Road have recently discovered that they are distantly related, having put together their genealogy with the help of family stories handed down by Orphea's great-aunts, Minerva and Cleopatra Proud. Raynor is the son of Mrs. Lola Grimes, an employee of Chaise and Sons Furniture Factory. Orphea and Raynor are shown here with Raynor's painting, "A Portrait of Lissa."*

■ ■ ■

Lola bought ten copies of the paper and gave three to me and the aunts. Aunt Cleo cut the article out and Aunt Minnie hung it over the counter.

"First time anybody in my family has ever made it in the paper. Fame! Nothing like it," Lola crowed.

■ ■ ■

We have the thickest, sweetest purple lilacs on either side of the store. They bloomed and bloomed that spring. Even Aunt Cleo had to admit they went well with the new yellow paint job. The straw man came from the paper factory to make the delivery so that we had straws to hand out with sodas, and toilet paper and paper towels to put on the shelves, and paper napkins to go with the sandwiches my aunts made to sell. The night before the delivery, Lola took off from work and permed her hair. It seems that once he'd made the delivery, the straw man was going over to Ray and Lola's house for dinner.

"Not as if she doesn't see him every chance she gets in town," Ray told me confidentially.

After the straw man made his delivery, a big order of canned goods arrived and some other stuff that Aunt Minnie had ordered from a catalog. Lola went to a neighbor's farm and brought us back some live chickens. Right on cue, the customers started coming. Until then, I hadn't known other people lived on the mountain.

"There are hollers around here," Ray explained. "Folks stay put in the bad weather. But then they stretch out of their homes. Kind of like bears."

"What do they do for a living?"

"Fix roofs, pick fruit, paint houses . . ."

I helped Aunt Minnie behind the counter, waiting on the customers. We averaged about eight per day. They came in all shapes, colors, and sizes. Each and every one of them noticed the newspaper clipping. Aunt Cleo thought it was good for business. But one day a man with a big bushy mustache started asking questions. "I hear that girl in the painting is queer. That true?"

I looked up in surprise. There was nothing like that in the newspaper caption.

"What if it is true?" growled Aunt Minnie. "Would that change the taste of this sandwich you ordered?"

"Expect not. But I don't believe in gays."

"And I don't believe in mustaches," she said, slamming his sandwich down.

He left the sandwich on the counter and walked out, muttering a cussword.

"Where did that come from?" Aunt Cleo asked with a sigh. "Somebody's been gossiping."

"Some folks don't have enough to occupy their minds," said Aunt Minnie. "Got to put their noses in other people's private lives." She patted me on the shoulder. "Don't let it worry you, honey child."

"I won't." But it did. What if because of me, Proud Store lost its few customers? For a few days, I was on edge. Thankfully, there wasn't another incident like that one.

■　■　■

Out of the blue one day, a couple came in and asked for a portrait! I didn't know what else to do so I took them over to see Ray. Right away they headed for Lissa. They'd seen her picture in the paper.

"She looks like she could walk right off the wall," said the woman.

"Very nice," said the man. He turned to Ray. "Think you could do something like that for us?"

"I ain't never done a portrait of people."

"But you did this girl on the wall."

"That was from a snapshot. I never painted from a live person."

"You can do it, Ray," I said.

"Nope, I can't."

"Come on, Ray. I dare you."

"We'll pay you five dollars," promised the man.

Ray's eyes popped. "In that case, I'll give it a shot."

He brought his paints and colored pencils and some paper over to the store. Do you know that boy did an awesome sketch of that couple in twenty minutes? They liked it a lot; maybe because the sketch made them look about ten years younger than they actually were. Ray was pleased, too, especially when they gave him the money. But when the couple was on their way out with the picture, he stopped them.

"Wait! She can write a poem for you."

"No, I can't. I don't write poems for people."

"You write them all the time about Lissa," said Ray.

"The lady and gentleman do not want to have a poem about themselves!"

"Sure we do," said the man, settling back. He and his wife ordered two ham sandwiches and some sodas from Aunt Minerva and paid Aunt Cleo at the register. I sat down with a pad and pencil. I hardly knew where to begin. I didn't know a thing about them. I finally hit upon a short format:

> *You climbed the mountain*
> *Your faces lifted*
> *Lovebirds fly home with full stomachs*

They gave me a dollar for it.

Suddenly Ray and I were in business. People were coming up the mountain for a portrait and a poem. We settled on a price of $5.50 for the set. Ray was very good at the portraits. This particular poetry that I was writing then—I wouldn't want you to judge me on it. After all, these were quickies. But here are a few of my better ones:

> *Though you bury the dead*
> *You are very well read*
> *The sun also rises in China*

I wrote that for Mrs. Graves when she came back a second time. I heard her tell Aunt Minerva that she wanted to go on vacation—that's where the part about China came from. I wanted her to go someplace really different.

Once a young couple brought their baby with them. They wanted Ray to paint the baby's picture, but she wouldn't keep still. So the whole family had to be in the portrait. Ray painted them eating tuna fish because that's what they'd ordered from Aunt Minerva.

A family hike
Preserved forever
Somewhere is a school of dolphins

Somewhat obscure, I know . . .

One day the mail carrier wanted his portrait and poem just like all the other folks. This particular guy wore two pairs of glasses at the same time, one pair on his nose and the other pair on top of his head. Aunt Minerva explained that one was probably for reading the names on the letters and the other pair was for distance while he was driving. I thought he looked like a Cyclops.

Master of the mountain
You have the Cyclops eye
Barking dogs flee in the distance

I gave it to him for free, since he didn't seem to like it. He didn't get the part about the barking dogs; how he didn't have to worry about them like mail carriers always do, because even a dog would be scared of those glasses. In any case, he was crazy about Ray's portrait.

Around that time I got a note from Marilyn telling me that Club Nirvana was open. She and Icky invited me to come up. They wanted me to perform my poetry and anything else I wanted to.

I explained about Marilyn and Icky to my aunts and told them about the poems I owed them. By this time, I had written a lot of stuff. The idea had been taking shape inside me that I could turn the material into a show, a show with poems in it. I would dedicate the show to Lissa. But now that it seemed like the show could become a reality, I got cold feet.

"I'm calling Marilyn and Icky and telling them I can't come."

"Are you sure?" asked Aunt Minnie. "Maybe it's time you had some fun, child. You told us about that open mike you used to go to."

"I haven't done that in so long. Besides, everything I've written lately is about Lissa and me and how we fell in love. I can't share that with anybody."

"Why on earth not?" said Aunt Cleo. "I'm sure your poetry is good."

"Lissa might not want me to talk about what happened between us in public."

"Well then, make your show about something else. You owe it to yourself to carry on. Or do you want to spend your whole life with Ray as the only company your age? We want you to do things with your life, Orphea. Don't you want to go back to school?"

"Yes, but I'd like to go down here. I'm not sure about doing the show in Queens."

I asked Ray to help me decide. We locked ourselves up in the root cellar and I read him what I'd written.

"What do you think?" I asked when I was done. "Is it stupid or what?"

Ray tossed his hair out of his eyes. "It's art."

"What do you mean?"

"It's *art*. Don't act like I'm simple."

"I'm not acting like you're simple. I just want you to explain."

"It's art like my paintings of Saint, like my portrait of Lissa. You didn't judge me and I'm not judging you."

"That means you don't like what I wrote."

He stamped his foot. "I didn't say that. I like it a lot."

"What do you like about it?"

"I like it because it sounds true."

But I decided not to do the show. I just couldn't.

My seventeenth birthday came and went. There was no word from Rupert and Ruby, which I took as a good sign. Aunt Minnie made me a birthday cake. It had eighteen candles on top. One for good luck. Ray, Lola, and the straw man came over. Lissa and I had always been the same age. Now I would always be older.

There is a run of mint in our garden
Holding back the fallen leaves
Yesterday I saw a footstep there
Just your size
I tracked you
To a well and peered down
The sight of a bucket to pull
Made me thirsty
So I filled it with water
Instead of seeing your face reflected
The face I saw on the surface was mine
When I am old a part of me
Will always be sixteen

SAVED

You're probably thinking the show should be over. But how did we get to Club Nirvana? I can't leave that part out. If you want to know, it started with a preacher named Isaiah Robinson.

■ ■ ■

Isaiah Robinson, the preacher, is Rupert's distant cousin on his mother's side. I didn't know all that when he came to the store. Isaiah is young with big muscles, smooth cheeks, great cologne, and an incredible rumbling voice, which gives him an air of authority beyond his years. When he stopped by, Aunt Cleo and Aunt Minerva really put the dog on for him: homemade peach pie with peach ice cream. I'm kind of skittish when it comes to preachers; probably some buried memory of the backs of my knees sticking to the front pew in Daddy's church for the first seven years of my life. But this guy was genuinely friendly. He seemed to know all about me, for some reason.

"I bet you're a literary type." He had a roguish gleam in his eye.

"I do write poetry."

"I do a lot of writing myself, preparing sermons and such. I'm working on one inspired by the prodigal son. Familiar with the parable?"

"Sure."

"A wandering child pops up on his family's doorstep, and the entire community celebrates the visit. That's why I'm here today," said Isaiah, "to invite you to the Homecoming."

"Homecoming?"

"Minnie and I go every year," Aunt Cleo chimed in. "Lola gives us a ride."

"This year I'll go with you, then."

"Folks will be glad to welcome you," said Isaiah, cutting his pie carefully. "You're famous, you know. You were in the newspaper."

■ ■ ■

The day of the Homecoming was a peak day in terms of nature: flowers bloomed along the road, birds chirped, and I'd never seen so many butterflies. As Ray helped me settle my aunts in the back of Lola's car along with the baskets of food they were bringing for the supper after the Homecoming service, I felt as cheerful as one of Aunt Minnie's new chicks. After months of mourning Lissa, a dark cloud was beginning to lift.

Going to church was exciting not because it was church, actually, but because there were so many people. Over the winter it had begun to feel as if my two aunts, Ray, Lola, and I were the only inhabitants in the world. Things had picked up when customers began coming to the store, especially after we went into the portrait and poetry business. But the Homecoming was something else again! The parking lot was packed to overflowing and young and old were dressed in their best. Folks' relatives had come from all over the country for the occasion. Aunt Cleo and Aunt Minnie were beaming. It was the first time in years they'd had another family member attending the service. Even Ray, who had gone along to help out with Aunt Cleo's chair, looked excited, though he did opt for hanging out in the car while the four of us went into church.

The church building itself was so sweet and small, with polished dark wood walls and windows banked with fragrant red lilies. Everybody in the world seemed to be nodding our way. We stopped in a room in back of the chapel that was set with long tables, so that Aunt Minnie could drop off her food. The spread was out of sight, roasts and chickens and dishes of vegetables and macaroni and cheese and fifty or sixty cakes and pies. The smell of it all! My stomach was rumbling—you get the idea. When I snuggled down next to Aunt Minnie in the fourth pew, I felt so at home. I was sitting in the very same church that Nadine had come to when she was a little girl, where she had sung "His Eye Is on the Sparrow" in the choir. And when Isaiah Robinson got up into the pulpit, I surprised myself by thinking of Daddy, and how he'd once been a young preacher standing in that very spot. I rested my head on Aunt Minnie's shoulder and Aunt Cleo squeezed my hand. I glanced over my shoulder to the back of the church and caught sight of Lola, her elbow leaning against one of the flower-laden windowsills.

Then in one of the very front pews on the other side of the church, I saw the back of a very familiar neck. It was during Isaiah's sermon. At first I couldn't believe it—Rupert was there! Nodding to beat the band, testifying under his breath, muttering something that sounded like "Preach it, man!"

Isaiah had gotten to the high point about the prodigal son's big celebration when Rupert twisted his neck around and stared. His eyes looked beady with meanness. Sweat popped out all over me. I felt like I might faint. How could he be there? I'd felt so safe. There hadn't been a word from him or Ruby. I'd tricked my-self into believing that I never had to see them again. A panicky feeling rose up inside of me. Rupert kept staring at me, which made the people sitting next to him turn and stare, too. I glanced around for an escape but I was pinned into the pew between Aunt Minnie and six other people on one side, and on the other side Aunt Cleo's wheelchair. Rupert stopped staring for a minute and turned around. I fanned myself with a church program. Aunt Minnie and Aunt Cleo hadn't a clue about what was happening; Aunt Minnie's eyes were glued to Isaiah and Aunt Cleo had her eyes closed while she swayed back and forth to the rhythm of the choir's background music. I glanced back to catch Lola's eye, but she, too, was captivated by the sermon. So I settled back and tried to relax. Maybe I wasn't the reason Rupert had come to the Homecoming; after all, his mother was from Handsome Crossing. It still seemed suspicious, though, because I'd never known him to go before. Seeing him brought back the rage in his voice on the morning Lissa died; my face experi-enced a visceral memory of his fist. I gazed up at the preacher for some kind of rescue. Though I wasn't quite sure what God thought of me, I was pretty cer-tain He wouldn't let Rupert beat me up again, espe-cially not in a packed church.

Then came the part where Isaiah began saving folks. The sermon was over and the choir was hum-ming loudly. Isaiah had his arms out and folks came straggling forward. I saw a woman whisper in his ear. He hugged her and said a prayer over her.

"Come and unburden yourselves, children," he invited us all. "Come home to the place where all is forgiven."

Rupert turned around again and started eyeballing me. I did my best to ignore him. But it was impossible, especially when Isaiah asked if there was anyone else who needed guidance and my brother announced in a very loud voice:

"Save my sister, Orphea!"

Aunt Minnie sat up and Aunt Cleo's eyes popped open. Everybody in the whole church turned to me. No wonder—Rupert was pointing his finger at me! The organ began to play faster and faster and the choir kept on humming. I felt myself becoming smaller and smaller. Then Isaiah Robinson called my name.

"Come, Orphea. Don't be afraid."

I was like a deer caught in headlights. Then the choir began singing "His Eye Is on the Sparrow," reminding me of Nadine.

I stuck my tongue out at Rupert and hopped over Aunt Cleo's wheelchair, hightailing it down the aisle to a chorus of amens. I don't know about you, but I think a person has the right to decide for herself if she needs to be saved.

My brother followed me out into the parking lot.

"Just a minute. What's your rush?"

"Leave me alone! Why are you here?"

"It was my duty to come down," he said, catching

up with me, "when I heard about that picture in the newspaper."

"What about it?"

His eyes narrowed. "Told you to be quiet about that. Might as well be taking out an ad for your next girlfriend."

"Get a life, Rupert! Nobody here gives a damn."

"People aren't as stupid as you think, Orphea. They put two and two together. Isaiah sent me a copy of the news clipping."

"And you filled him in?"

"It was my duty. He's your preacher."

"I hardly know the man! All you did is humiliate me again, Rupert—that's what you did. I'm seventeen now. I don't need you controlling my life."

"Like hell you don't! I'm your guardian. I was wrong to think the old ladies would set you straight."

"What's that supposed to mean?"

"You can change," he said, stepping up closer. "You blew it today in the church but you still have a chance."

"I am who I am, Rupert. You might as well try to change a can of potted meat into a can of tuna."

"Told you we don't have those kind of people in our family," he growled, grabbing me by the collar. "You're going home with me right this minute."

"I'm not!" I screamed. "Let go!"

He tried to drag me. I struggled against him.

One second I saw Ray crouched on top of a car. The next second he was on Rupert's back, yanking at his hair and kicking him.

"Get off, you simpleton!" Rupert screamed. "Get off!"

By now people were running out of the church, Isaiah and Lola in front.

"What's the disturbance here?" Isaiah's voice boomed out.

"What are you doing, Ray Grimes?" shrieked Lola.

Rupert had fallen on his knees while Ray clung to his neck fiercely.

"Get this fool off me! He's choking me."

"It's okay, Ray!" I cried.

Ray hopped up abruptly and Rupert fell face-first onto the ground. "Oh, my God!" He grabbed his mouth. "That fool chipped my tooth!"

Some folks in the crowd started tittering, but most just shook their heads. Isaiah came forward to help Rupert. He led him back into the church.

"Let's go home," said Aunt Minerva.

Aunt Cleo looked back longingly. "Without supper?"

"I made some extra and left it home. There's been enough excitement for one day."

When he got into the car, Ray was grinning. "Did you see me, Orphea?"

"Yeah, Ray. You really did ride him."

■　■　■

That day changed my mind about going to Queens. I would perform the show I'd been writing and dedicate it to Lissa.

But I didn't want to go by myself. I wanted Ray to go with me.

"What would I do in the big city?" he said stubbornly.

"See the sights. We could go to an art museum. You could even be part of the show."

"Doing what?"

"Painting."

"I don't paint in front of people."

"You paint in front of me all the time."

"That's different."

"Come on, Ray. I need you. I might be afraid up there all by myself."

"Will we get paid? I'm thinking of saving my money up for a real horse."

"Icky and Marilyn already gave me two hundred dollars. I can give you some of that. Maybe we can even sell some of your paintings."

He smiled. "I'll go."

But we still had to talk Lola into it.

"How are you going to get there?"

"We can take the bus. I'll pay for Ray's ticket."

"I'd have to talk to the club owners."

"We can call them."

"Ray's only fourteen."

"For Pete's sake, Mama!" Ray snapped. "You don't expect me to spend the rest of my life in a root cellar, do you?"

"Of course not, sweet pea." She turned to me with a worried expression. "How long will you be gone?"

"Just for the summer."

"You won't let anything happen to my boy in the big city?"

"I'll take care of him," I promised.

"We'll take care of each other," said Ray.

I called Icky and Marilyn. The next week Lola drove Ray and me into town and we got on a bus.

■ ■ ■

The trip only took took seven hours. I slept most of the way but Ray was wired. He had to get off at every rest stop to try some new brand of cupcake or soda. And he wouldn't stop staring.

"People are going to think you're loony," I warned. But a lady with a baby across the aisle from us seemed to like him. When the baby wouldn't stop fussing, the lady gave him to Ray to hold. The baby was cooing in no time, though he did pull Ray's hair.

When we got off the bus in Manhattan, I think we both needed a shower. The air conditioner on the bus had stopped working. Marilyn was there to meet us and we went on a subway. The crowds and the noise might have made Ray feel a bit timid. I kind of had to hold his hand. But by the time we'd been in New York for a week, Ray was galloping down Queens Boulevard.

Putting the show together with Icky and Marilyn was the most exciting thing that's ever happened to me. It was Marilyn who helped me string all my writing together. Icky concentrated on the set and the lights and buying materials for Ray.

Except for the fact that I kept forgetting what I was supposed to say, the rehearsals seemed to go okay. Then one day Marilyn yelled at me.

"Stop turning around!"

Just like in the root cellar, I'd been watching Ray.

"I'm just making sure he isn't painting too many horses," I explained.

"Can I paint at least one horse?" Ray whined.

"Maybe one."

Marilyn chuckled. "We'll call the show 'Not a Rodeo' just to remind him."

"Keep your eyes on the audience, Orphea," Icky directed from the booth. "We'll make it a rule that you can't turn around."

Opening night came. The crowd was much smaller than today, yet I was so nervous. But as I started to tell the story, I got a warm feeling inside. People were listening.

Next week Lola and the straw man are driving up! They're staying with us a couple of days in Icky and Marilyn's loft.

I wish Aunt Minnie and Aunt Cleo could come see us. But they're keeping it together at home.

"When you have a store, you can't go out of town," said Aunt Minnie.

"Confining," said Aunt Cleo. "But we love it."

■　■　■

So that's our show. Me running my mouth a mile a minute, and Ray painting a canvas that only you see. Even when it's over, I don't turn around. Things are going so well, I don't want to jinx them. There's magic in the air here. I think the magic comes from the audience. You never know who'll show up. Last week after the show, Lissa's sister, Annie, came up to me outside. It was a shock. We both cried. She's living out in Brooklyn. I'm going to try to see her before we go back to Proud Road.

Now I have a fantasy that Lissa will walk into the club one day; that she didn't die. She'll pass the club and see my show being advertised, and come that same evening just like Annie did; sit right down and watch the show and go absolutely nuts about Ray's painting. She'll hug me and the next day we'll take Ray to a big museum. Only a fantasy . . . I saw the urn with her ashes.

But if this were a fairy tale or a myth, she might materialize out of Ray's canvas and be standing behind me . . . a girl with thick black hair and gray eyes.

You know the myth about the guy named Orpheus? The one Nadine named me for? He was a great poet and singer. The love of his life gets bitten by some sort of snake and she dies. But Orpheus goes after her, straight to the underworld. He almost gets to bring her home. But the deal is that he can't turn around. Just as they're about to step back on earth, Orpheus gets nervous and takes a peek. The love of his life disappears, lost to him forever.

If Lissa were behind me right now, I wouldn't turn around for a million bucks. I would keep my promise not to look back. She would step out of Ray's painting and follow me offstage and out of Club Nirvana. Even though my arms would throb with the urge to give her a hug, I'd resist. Just knowing that she was a step behind me would be enough. I'd feel her breath on my neck and take in the fragrance of peanut butter, lemons, and patchouli.

The truth is I'm the one who comes alive, when I step onto the stage to tell you I've been loved. I feel you listening. I feel them, too—the ones who loved me—somewhere deep inside. Breathing, if only for a little while.

> *Pebble smooth, found in snow*
> *Finger pricked the blood that flowed*
> *With parched tongue, I sing you*
> *Ocean's mist, our first kiss*
> *Hot ice*
> *Taboo to the touch*
> *Fire in the cold*
> *Us*

Thanks for coming!

Let's give it up for painter Raynor Grimes!

On lights, Mr. Icarus Digits!

Your waitress and sometime bass player,
    Marilyn Chin!

You're a great audience!

See you on the street.

ABOUT THE AUTHOR

Commended by *Publishers Weekly* for her "compassionate rendering of contemporary families," Sharon Dennis Wyeth is the author of *The World of Daughter McGuire* and *A Piece of Heaven,* a New York Public Library Book for the Teen Age. Her picture book *Something Beautiful* and her historical novel *Freedom's Wings* are both NCSS-CBC Notable Children's Trade Books in the Field of Social Studies. *Once on This River,* set in the African American community of colonial New York, has been among the New York Public Library's 100 Titles for Reading and Sharing. Another picture book, *Always My Dad,* is a *Reading Rainbow* Selection. Sharon Dennis Wyeth graduated cum laude from Harvard University and is a former faculty member of the New School for Social Research. She has been a keynote speaker at the annual conference of the International Reading Association and a recent guest of the National Library in Iceland.

Sharon Dennis Wyeth lives with her family in Upper Montclair, New Jersey.